D0596448

Betrayed by
F. Scott Fitzgerald

Betrayed by
F. Scott Fitzgerald

A NOVEL BY

Ron Carlson

W · W · Norton & Company · New York · London

First published as a Norton Paperback 1984

COPYRIGHT © 1977 BY RON CARLSON

Library of Congress Cataloging in Publication Data

Carlson, Ron.

Betrayed by F. Scott Fitzgerald.

I. Title.

PZ4.C2854Be3 [PS3553.A733] 813'.5'4 77-3320

ISBN 0-393-30168-0

All Rights Reserved

Published simultaneously in Canada
by Stoddart, a subsidiary of General
Publishing Co. Ltd, Don Mills, Ontario

This book was designed by Antonio Krass
Typefaces used are Bernhard Modern Roman and Avanta
Manufacturing was done by Haddon Craftsmen

Printed in the United States of America
2 3 4 5 6 7 8 9 0

For Georgia Elaine

———————————————

Everything that glitters should be gold.

Eldon Robinson-Duff

My undergraduate days, having left my bed and board, I can no longer be responsible for their debts.

Larry Boosinger
Daily Utah Chronicle

Betrayed by
F. Scott Fitzgerald

1

"Blame is not important," my father used to say. "Whose fault it is will not get anything fixed." And he ran a benevolent household wherein no one cried over spilled anything, providing the offender sprang up to get a towel. I'd always shared a vague inclination toward this pragmatism, until several grown men spilled everything everywhere in my name and did less than nothing toward clearing it up. The days before we learn the value of revenge are callow days indeed. In the mirror today darker eyes than I have ever known are reflected, and I have reluctantly become the kind of man who waits suspiciously in hotel rooms for the safe arrival of his luggage.

I should add that I do not blame Fat Nicky, the Waynes, Teeth, exclusively, nor Lila, Royal, or any of the host of citizens, attorneys, Indians, housewives, turnkeys who have hounded and disappointed me, and in the end committed indelibilities upon my tabula somewhat rasa, but I do blame

11

them for generous portions of it. In reflection I have walked these routes again and again like a rabid mailman and it keeps coming up the same: bad news. I am not of so wishy-washy a temperament as to call myself an innocent bystander, "There are no innocent victims," Sartre said; but I was clearly a bystander, amazed that people seemed to be doing things to me, or ignoring me, all on purpose. The acts I did commit, stemming as they did from creeds outworn and untenable obsessions, were perhaps for the most part exactly wrong. From where I sit tonight, by a river full of the season's first fallen leaves, talking quietly with a woman with whom it seems a future might be founded, these recent calamities, these recent wins, losses, ties, appear in mind as a berserk sort of shuffleboard, the scores lost in retrospect.

2

I knew myself. Let's spend the largest lies at the beginning. But despite this dizzying self-knowledge, I was happy when events took a sudden manual turn, when the allegorical fistfight my life had been became more like the genuine article and people began hurling more than words at each other.

We were playing drunken croquet at DeLathaway's on the first springlike evening of the year, and I, being the only person present still in some touch with his reflexes, was winning. DeLathaway was from Maryland, and went around generally pretending to be decadent and from the Deep South, honing his accent in his poetry class, and this bourbon-and-croquet thing was his idea of the way a lost southern aristocrat entertains.

I had spent the first hour drinking Old Bardstown Kentucky Bourbon Whiskey, made in Bardstown, Kentucky, 86 proof, reading the bottle labels, and trying to figure out why I had been invited. As I counted heads, Wesson and I were the only two "students." Ah Wesson, who was presently standing on the porch talking Chaucer to DeLathaway, Wesson had finagled this, somehow inviting himself, and subsequently me, since he was afraid to attend any faculty social event alone.

Although DeLathaway did like me. I had taken his class and bought all his books, and I recall I was in my formal period, which lasted most of a semester, writing pattern poems about race-car driving and hunting with hounds, things I'd never done. (I hadn't done much, it was occurring to me). I thought DeLath was young to be so form oriented, he considered open verse to be as low as stealing hubcaps; "Scaly," he called it.

Even the croquet course was set up impeccably on his manicured lawn, on which, as I've noted, I was winning the ball game. By my return trip through the wickets, I had been delivered to that quasi-orbital, sour-mash precipice that has allowed me at other times to (1) put out entire tupperware parties with a single garden hose, women fleeing the patio in every compass direction, covering their heads with lettuce crispers; (2) present my "Vietnam is not over" address to standing-room-only crowds at Arby's Roast Beef Sandwich Restaurant; (3) and casually board passing trains. That is to say I was moving into the margins, mallet in hand: belligerency in chinos.

"Larry. Hey, Larry Boosinger." Banks, who teaches Shakespeare, *and* had graced my most recent adventure-in-sight—a paper on the strength of the puns in King Lear—with a D, was calling me aside in his inebriated sotto voce.

I walked over to where he leaned on DeLathaway's junked '57 Buick, the kind with the three snazzy holes in the side. The

Buick was sitting on four cinder blocks in the driveway, head-lights broken out, and weeds grew up through the floorboards. There were no doors and DeLath kept a ratty, runty goat tied to the back bumper. I had already pointed out that his "Deep South" focus was confused, by the contrast the wreck made against his well-kept lawn and the four huge Dorian columns that supported his tiny porch gable.

"Order, yes," DeLathaway had said and pointed to the car, "But ma Buke is a *classic.*"

Banks stood leaning on the ruin, and I sat up on the fender next to him, absolutely awash, and said, "Yeah, Banquo?"

He did a little backward blink, and it didn't register in my engorged mind that no one had ever called him that to his face. But he recovered, frowned, and came closer.

"Listen, Boosinger, this girl," he indicated a blonde, Susette Bedd, one of the department secretaries, who was groping for her ball under an azalea. While we were watching she fell down twice. "This girl, she should win." He put his hand over his mouth, inadvertently covering his nose too; the gesture was to indicate enough said.

"Right, Mr. Banks."

"Right, then. Right." He smiled at me and fell into the driver's seat.

I went back to my ball: I was orange. No one was paying a whole lot of attention to the game; there wasn't much con-sciousness left, but when someone would knock someone else into the shrubbery, a perfectly legal tactic, cries of indignation fired out into the twilight. Royal, a fine Milton scholar who had been at the university so long that the paper cover of *The Great Gatsby* had changed four times, was blasted into the neighbor's yard by Virgil Benson, the film instructor. It was really a very logical, objective stroke, but Royal screamed and his eyes boiled up.

Wesson, my pal, leaped off the porch where he had just said, "Why, there's not a single black man in all of Chaucer!" in an overloud, point-getting voice to DeLathaway. The two of them, Wesson and his teacher, Royal, surrounded Benson in a scene straight out of *Riders of the Purple Sage,* in its push-shove possibilities. The trio shuffled about for a moment, then Benson apologized to Royal, quietly dropped out of the game, and went to the backyard where the wives had circled DeLa-thaway's ten-ton rusted wrought-iron lawn furniture and were holding court. Watching Virgil Benson place his mallet in the rack touched me. I liked Benson. He showed *Frankenstein* a lot, and shared a sympathy for the monster that I found to be the closest thing to truth in the university. Royal brought his green ball back in bounds, and gave himself a favorable lie. I made up my mind to get him.

Confusion, like Koko, the albino horse-riding bear that appears in the circus wearing red scarves and leaping through flames, was mounting. DeLathaway had fallen off the porch and was wriggling in the pyracantha. When everyone rushed up to help him, I saw the secretary Susette lift her blue ball out of the shrubbery surreptitiously and flip it halfway home. I decided, regardless of Banquo, to get her too. DeLath was laughing now from where he lay in the bushes, and intoned: "A bed of roses, a bed of thorns, a bed of roses . . ." while a relatively nincompoopal crowd looked on from the porch.

Royal stood by his green ball, crooning now into the microphone of his mallet: "It was only a Tristram in old Shanty town . . ." He kept singing it over and over to make sure everyone would hear it, which they already had. I figured he must really be in the throes of Old Bardstown to be attempting the first joke of his entire life. People looked at him strangely until he dropped the mallet and stood leaning on it sheepishly. And meanwhile, hearing Royal sing, Banks had begun bellowing from his seat in the Buick, "Desdemona! Where the hmmm hmmm hhmm hmmm hmmm hmmm hmmm!" to the tune of "Oklahoma," but this too stopped after a dozen birds scattered from their nests in the headlights and Wesson ran over to see if Banks was okay. You can tell when jokes aren't funny if you begin considering crying for your enemies.

I felt a little sorry for Royal. All he really wanted out of life was a comfortable room lined with unopened leatherbound copies of the rare books of the Western World, in which he and a few friends, a ruly, polite group, could sip tea and play intense marathon games of Authors.

Amid this display of sound and senselessness, and despite two onlookers, Professors Keen and Roachfield standing nearly on top of me discussing the merits of the first versus the third person, I whacked my orange ball out of turn. I did. Thus on my next turn, with the whole world watching, I tapped old orange cleanly through the double hoops and became Poison.

"He's Poison!" Miss Bedd said.

Royal executed the frown he'd made famous in forty yearbooks.

Upon hearing the word, "Poison" the entire sodden community emerged to take a look. DeLathaway, now on the porch, scratched but smiling, rubbed his hands together as if to say, "Ah yes, on with the games." Banquo sat up in the Buick, as I feared he would, and did several neck-jarring takes. Wesson looked worried. He skipped over to me, not being too obvious, because he wanted to be seen mostly talking to teachers, not "candidates," which we both were.

"Caution, Lawrence."

"Larry, Wesson; and why?"

"It's a faculty party, remember. We're *guests.*" He wiggled his tie.

"I'm Poison, Wesson, one side please, or you may find yourself comatose at this particular faculty party." He skulked away.

After I sent orange ball into the field, at large, and the turns
rotated, Banks motioned to me.

"You fool!" he said, gripping the steering wheel of the Buick
in an isometric demonstration that bulged his temples.

"Easy there, fella."

"Easy! Why did you do that! Now you're going to have to
aim for one of the hoops and disqualify yourself. Right?"

"Right, uh huh, right, right. Right, Mr. Banks." While
self-destruction was to become much more my style on future
days, this hurling myself through a hoop business would not go.
I returned to the wickets. I decided to venomize Royal first;
and in obviously the best shooting of the evening I reached out
and nailed him with a tricky forty-foot putt.

"Death to Sir Green," I said. "Touché, Messr. Royal."

"Why you've poisoned me!"

"Yes and I've taken your class." His jaw descended as an
invitation to a left hook and I imagined my arm swinging
across, clearing the air. But I simply added: "Zounds!"

He stomped off, into the backyard. Wesson walked at his
side, picking up his mallet, muttering rapidly, being generally
attendant, the squire that he was.

"Now, Miss Blue, for your dosage, arm or cheek?" Susette
used her turn to flee, but unfortunately right into a small ditch
that circled DeLathaway's new weeping willow. Banks was
really paying attention now, on the edge of his seat, rapt say.
So I simply said, "Drink this then to me, dear, and sweets,
don't-you-know, to the you-know-who." And I sent the potent
orange right into the ditch as well, where it kissed blue for the
last time.

"Ahhhh!" Banks screamed in anguish. Susette was pouting,

luckily, and so his attentions were shifted to her, his wife being in the backyard. I escaped to the porch where DeLathaway kissed both cheeks and knighted me with my own mallet.

"This boy," he said to Virgil Benson, who had been driven back out of the backyard as well, "is going to be as great a poet as he is a croquet player."

"No doubt." Virgil said quietly.

"Why do you realize he has already written a perfect sestina?" It was true. For some reason I had written one in one of my crossword moods, but it wasn't perfect.

"Whiskey! We need more whiskey."

"No, thanks DeLath," I said. "I have to meet Riddel at the Black Heron and give him my last paper." Riddel taught a philosophy course I was taking as allied studies, and had given me ten extra days on my paper which lay freshly typed on the seat of my green pickup even as I spoke. "And I have to be at work by twelve midnight." I checked my watch: three o'clock. That meant it was eleven, my watch having been four hours fast for a year. Virgil Benson left, in order to get home in time for the late show, no doubt.

"Naw. N-O. You are the champion and deserve to be celebrated. Come on to the back." On the way through the kitchen, a man smiled and handed me a drink. He was Leeland Rose, DeLathaway's "help," and I've yet to figure out if his smile indicated that he knew we'd both be dangerous convicts soon, playing baseball on another side of the bars; there are so many different smiles in this world.

"Haven't you always thought it curious the way we say, 'Fix a drink,' as though it were broken," Delathaway was saying, always the student of poetic idiom, raking the language for oddities. He looked at the ceiling and lit one of his famous cigars.

As he exhaled acres of smoke upward and stood studying it, I reeled into the backyard, surprising my vertebrae by missing three stairs. "Leeway, here," I whispered, getting up, "Degree candidate in need of leeway."

Wesson was now nodding wild affirmation into Professor Roachfield's face as the latter offered his new theories on drama. I heard my earnest friend ask the professor, "You mean, if the playwright shows us the gun in Act One, he now has the responsibility *not* to fire it in Act Three? My God! that's amazing!"

I passed them and joined Professor Keen, an intense comparative-lit teacher, who was sitting aside the main circle of wives. The wives were talking about the history department wives. As I sat down by Keen, I didn't know what to expect, from him or myself. He was esoteric and intense, and I was still buzzing. Keen had the quality I'd noticed lately in Wesson of going around as though every day was the one before the Graduate Record Exam, asking everyone large questions and then looking at his watch. He had stopped me one day in the hall and asked, "In total, would you say Melville or Faulkner is the greatest American writer?"

I'd made him a permanent enemy by answering, "Faulkner by land, Melville by sea." Tonight, he appeared a bit more mellow, having just published an article in *Overview* on how Spanish gothic novels caused American southern gothic novels, though I did sense an aura of antagonism because I had blitzed Royal's chances on the hoops of praise; but, Keen asked instead, "Who's your favorite writer, Boosinger?"

"Burroughs."

"Really?" Keen looked up from the blade of grass he was splitting into tenths. "Why he's quite difficult isn't he? Obscure, arbitrary, wild?"

"Yes sir, quite difficult, but it pays off."

"Hmmm. Well, do you think his latest work compares with the early stuff, say *Naked Lunch?*"

"Keep William S., Keen. I'm talking about the prolific Edgar Rice, and yes, I think *Tarzan and the Antmen* and *Tarzan Goes to Mars* compare quite favorably with say, *Tarzan* and *Tarzan and the Apes.*"

Keen was pretty obviously recoiling at what he recognized as my potential to do him bodily you know what, so I asked him, "Do you think French bad taste compares to American bad taste?" I left him there, frightened in the dark, rubbing his chin.

Darkness had fallen and the backporch beacon and my unsteady head made the whole scene seem a black and white film shot with a hand-held camera, the tripod gone to hell, and the cameraman away at the races. The circle of women had drawn closer and white light fringed their hair; white smoke rose from their Vantages, and their dark husbands knelt on the lawn between their chairs. I knew most of the wives and they were interesting taken one at a time, but "Faculty Wives" as a group and a concept are like a great heavyweight fighter: elusive, heavy, and repeatedly able to knock you down, if not out. All I could hear from the group was a few proper nouns and they were all names of women and cities in Europe: Daphne, Cleo, Doris, Dover, Marseilles, Naples. It was time, as it had been for three hours, for me to get out. A cool hand fell on my arm. It was Mrs. Banks. "I hear you won the croquet. Congratulations."

"Thanks, Mrs. Banks." I said, burning at how incredibly silly it sounded, especially to this woman whom I had enjoyed watching in her husband's otherwise disappointing class. She thought, as she should I suppose, that Banks was a genius because he actually taught Shakespeare and had a few ideas of his own. Banks was one of the department's youngest appointees, and that, along with the fact that he played handball with key department figures, made her complexion even rosier as she basked in the warming envy of greying wives. She must have known though, regardless of their relatively darling position, that she was married to a dolt. She had sat in on our class from time to time, sitting over one and up two seats from me, rubbing her cheerful little breasts against the edge of the desk, as I ran my hands along the edge of my own.

I asked her why she hadn't played croquet and things began to grow rapidly, like those weeds that took over the world in *Day of the Triffids*, out of control. She came back and sat by me away from the central pow-wow, and I was telling her about my deep desires to drive race-cars and hunt with hounds and really ride the rodeo. She was fascinated, and full of Dubonnet, and leaned quite towards me, when Royal decided to test my bellicosity by pouring his drink on my head saying, "There! I'll dilute thy vile poison, I'll nullify thy sting." He was really gone.

"The hell, Mister," I said as I introduced his Roman nose to fist city. Then the imitable Wesson was on my back and I was yelling let go or I'd let flee a fart. Finally, after a very strenuous neck-wringing moment, I hurled him onto Keen, deciding not to rehabilitate either of them, and spat out: "Zane Grey, Edgar Rice, Gifford Pinchot, Edward Stratemeyer!" I didn't remember who Pinchot was, but I think he was one of Teddy Roosevelt's friends, so he'd be all right, and Stratemeyer wrote *Rover Boys Beat the Nazis* and a million et ceteras.

Then I was lost for several jungle seconds in DeLathaway's landscape foliage, and Mrs. Banks—whom I was calling Adele by now—appeared and escorted me to a very stimulating form of safety behind the garage. For a minute I regretted being so drunk, and Adele was hurrying many things.

The next image that registered was a closeup of Banks himself, leering into the backseat of the Buick, where I found the vinous Adele pretending I was her desk. From where I sat I seemed to be cooperating. Banks was bellowing and hitting the top of the car with my croquet mallet which was doing quite the job on one of my five senses. DeLathaway's goat was scared and had run to the end of the rope nearly throttling itself, crying a high goat bleat in time with Bank's insane drumming. This is the end of the world, I thought, bangs *and* whimpers, and leaving Adele, nipples atwitter, I exited the automobile, cut the goat's tether, and as it ran wild circles eating at the rest of the rope, I boarded my green pickup. Banquo was close behind, playing a rampant imagined game of polo with my head. I peeled out. Poor Banks, I thought, smelling his wife on my hands, his sons will be kings.

3

The Black Heron will remain for many years a sociologist's Disneyland. For years it had been a small bar, The Lilac Playroom, a rendezvous for passed-over whores, spent jockeys, and deathbound vagrants. Then, in my sophomore year, when the Old Black Heron located a block up the street was torn down to make a parking lot of Ashley-Wasatch Industries (a budding branch of the newly formed Indian mafia), the Black Heron bought out The Lilac Playroom, and all the bright, rosy, saddle-shoed sophomores started dropping in. The old crowd stayed. So on any given night there they were, intellectuals all, creating in their curious merger an atmosphere redolent of Panama and Tivoli Reds, sequins and salvation armed Brooks Brothers, that was the exact chemistry necessary to spawn all the Alice Coopers this world needs. There was also, as I have hinted, a third group: hungry-looking men and women in short-sleeve white shirts carrying notebooks. Sociologists. That is, "degree candidates in the turbid, glacial world of sociology," without whose patronage the still purple Black Heron would have certainly floundered, as they were the heaviest drinkers.

Dr. Riddel always sat at the end of the bar, usually surrounded by his most ardent, dissolute students. They talked philosophy, Riddel always being the stable voice of genius, regardless of the amount of Black Velvet he consumed, and the students and former students moving in and out of beery euphoria as ideas assumed the personification only drink can bestow.

After fleeing DeLathaway's, I drove heedless of traffic lights down to the Black Heron listening to Dallas Levine sing, "Let Bygones by Bye-Bye-Bye Gones," hardly a good song, but I sang along anyway. When I got out of the truck, I found the orange mallet in the back; Banks must have thrown it eighty yards. Too much handball for that man.

I found Riddel unusually alone at the end of the bar. As our eyes met and instantly shared the camaraderie available only to those people who meet after an evening of drinking in different places, I handed him the paper. It was a simple thesis entitled "Philosophy of Disappearance." Riddel set the masterpiece in a beer ring on the bar.

"Is it true," he said, ignoring the fact that our relationship and its rights and responsibilities, debits and credits, had been terminated by the delivery of the manuscript, "that you're getting married?"

"Eventually. Where'd you hear that?"

"Dorothy came by earlier and made the announcement. Ah Larry, Larry I hate to see a lovely boy like you get married."

"Don't look. And besides don't worry; if I ever do it, it won't be to Dotty Everest." Dotty Everest, criminy, the world is full of dangerous characters. "Now, sir, do you want to talk about my paper?"

"No."

"Okay, then Riddel, it's been nice. Philosophy is real good. But watch out for my paper."

"Why?"

"Because it's real heavy." As I said that I noticed a smear of mustard on the cover sheet of the paper.

But I was an hour late for work, and my watch read five. I had one drink with Riddel, pretending in a way that this wasn't all past tense already, and then left him there alone. If he hadn't been so rich he would have been one of the greatest men in the Western World. He was one of the two geniuses I have ever known. It made me sad that here he was, the greatest man in the purple Black Heron, a man whose intelligence radiated like prepared uranium, enough to power a submarine, and it could no longer matter to me at all. He had been killed by his mother's money (she owned controlling interest in the Rolling Doughnut Company), and would spend his life in that bar, warming passers-by to undeserved promise. I only mention this at all here because Riddel's associate, a man named Darrel Teeth who was an ex-con (grand larceny) was to play a too integral part in a collision of miseries I was to have later.

When I got out to the power company where I was night-watchman, Eldon Robinson-Duff was there as I'd hoped he'd be. If I didn't come by the apartment by eleven-thirty for my keys, my stalwart roommate carried the mail.

Our relationship was well founded in eighth grade meta-phor: At midnight in the rain on a little runway in an un-charted portion of Mexico two men are having a fistfight on, under, and near a small weathered biplane. Though the fight is vigorous, the men are deliberate, slipping in the mud, each hauling the other up by the wet fur of his flight jacket and aiming each clear-fisted blow at the other's chin, trying for the knock out. They are fighting to prevent the other from taking off in this the worst storm of the season, a post-hurricanal squall known as Esmeralda. The message, something about the Zim-merman Letter, must be delivered. The two now wrestle under the fuselage, black in the mire and the night. If one of them hadn't shown up at the airstrip, the other would have flown up onto the mountains thinking forsaken thoughts about the ab-sentee. As is, one has won and drags the other out of the way, and wipes the unconscious face clean, propping him against a Yucca tree. Then the victor starts the little plane and launches into the buffeting winds wiping his goggles, determinedly watching for the harrow teeth mountains that pass like a razor through the air fifteen feet from his balloon tires. The pilot, I am saying, would be Eldon or me; the mud-man on the ground waving his fist and swearing into zeppelin clouds would be the same.

Plus, we fished together, and were aficionados of a sort that way. Now Eldon was lying on the floor reading *The New Yorker*, flipping his ashes into the pages. Sometimes at our apartment friends would pick up *Popular Mechanics* or the *Welding Journal*, the only two magazines we took, and a cupful of ashes would slide out onto their laps. Eldon looked up at me; behind him the vast computer board of the plant flashed the two hundred blue A-OK lights.

"Have you been," he asked, "seeing people socially?"

"Only the smallest tid-bits of it were social."

"Well, since you've arrived in time to avoid being fired, I suppose I'll go home and work." He got off the floor after putting his cigarette out on an ad for a polar bear carved in glass. "Oh, Lenore dropped by."

"Oh?"

"Yeah, remember, your betrothed."

"What did she say?"

"She was with Gary, the drugman."

"Pharmacy student. Yeah, well, what did she say?"

"She was mildly curious about what you're up to lately."

"What'd you say?"

"I told her I was no go-between."

"Shit, Eldon."

"What was I supposed to say, Larry? Christ. That you're conducting a noble experiment? That you have a dream?" He put on his red football helmet, and turned, showing a fist to me, simply, as a fact. "She's your girl. People who are engaged are supposed to see each other occasionally. Keep company, you know?"

"I don't know—I'm trying to do this thing right."

"Right! Ha! You haven't seen her for a month!"

"Twenty-two days, seven hours."

He looked at me from the depths of his helmet. "I'm going home to work. Don't forget that we were supposed to show the film tonight."

Robinson-Duff was always going home to work on his book. His motto was simply, "If you want to read a good book, you have to write it." After he left I strolled around the office for awhile, my head buzzing like a taut wire. This is a bun, I thought, I have a bun on. I wondered how much pharmacists earn. Outside the soundproof office, the two boilers, each as big

as houses, roared. Every twenty minutes or so they would kick
off and hum and tick for four or five minutes like an overheated
car, and then start up again, gaining momentum, building to
a stampeding blare. I thought about the girl I loved, Lenore.

We were supposed to become married when I finished the
degree in late August, and had tentatively set October 12,
Columbus Day, as the date. Did I add that she was perfect?
Oh not in the conventional sense of that word, but ideally,
perfect. Remembered names, played the piano delicately, became morally indignant once a week, was in her first year of
medical school, alluded to her girlhood in tense situations,
smelled wonderful at all times, read *all* of Zane Grey, and knew
how to fish expertly. These things, I thought sometimes looking at her soft, intelligent face incredulously, put her beyond
my comprehension. At first I thought she had been merely
titillated by motoring about with a madman, frightening clerks,
drinking warm vermouth from the bottle, and hiking along
little-known streams in the Uintas angling uncannily for ancient trout.

Then one euphoric evening in the Commercial Club in
Duchesne after a fishing trip, we became engaged. Immediately upon entering the place, I inadvertently sat on a runty
sheep-shearer who was sleeping something off in one of the
booths. He was so mad and disoriented and I was so embar-
rassed and surprised that we fought without even thinking
about it, tipping over two bar stools in the sluggish melee. I was
trying for a third or at least hoping to tip a table or break a
bottle, when he swallowed his chewing tobacco, and the con-
test was over as he stumbled retching toward the back door.
Then Lenore danced with her hero nine dances in a row to
Lester Kind's "Milktruck at Dawn," a blues number, I guess.
Everybody in the place was buying us drinks, and every once

in a while someone would fake a retch and laughter would fill the room and the barkeep would bring over two more glasses. Naturally, after that as we crossed the gravel parking lot, when I paused long enough to look into the laughing eyes of Lenore, I proposed, and she jumped into my arms placing the most memorable embrace of my life around my bruised self.

I had had The Thought first that night, driving down out of the mountains scanning a dozen deer in the headlights, braking to a sideward career, just short of the herd that stood curious as freshmen, then filed smooth as water over a fence, that I was not certain whether or not one marries that which is perfect. Seemed like openly asking for paradox to me. Also, one of the foremost considerations was a familiar quotation that floated about my mind in ready reach. My father had said it: "Marriage is compromise, Larry." And without stretching a thing I can add that I was (and still am in a sense) for keeping the edge of non-compromise sharp, a blade, don't you know it, that cuts both of the ways. Yes it does.

At eight by my watch, I checked the computer board, plugging in each room slide, reading temperatures in the spaces nearly a mile away, and making sure no one was in there stealing things. Then I logged the state computer board which was the easiest job, since each of the two hundred lights was always, unblinkingly blue, never orange. And as the alcohol rinsed my brain of any brain cells that weren't tied down, I tried to be clever and cryptic and Scott Fitzgerald into the massive log book.

"Four o'clock and all is well, power is being sent and received all over the state. Each house veritably hums with it. We, again, are lighting the dark night of the soul. There are a million volts going out, but never the same volt twice. Amps for the lamps of Salina, Moab, Kanab, and St. George, not to mention Bear River. Cordially, F. Scott Boosinger."

Mr. Proctor didn't like me going on like that in the log, "Just the facts, eh Boosinger?" he'd say. "Just the times and temperatures. We really don't want to know your every quirk. It isn't a personal diary, you know."

"Yes it is." I'd say. The date was printed in light blue letters at the top of every page, and the lower third of every page was designated in crisp light red letters: Graveyard Shift. I wrote in the fat leatherbound book every day, rather, night; it *was* my personal diary. Besides it was always interesting to go back three weeks and read my entries and wonder what rapacious humor had possessed my body then. I put the coffee on to boil and sat back down at the log, turning backward.

February 14: "How many people celebrate St. Valentine's by the Rhine? Wine, that is. Yes and before work, and with better company than these two snoring boilers, which, according to all computer feedback here on the dotted board—and if you are interested—seem to be functioning adequately. Yes, we have no oranges. Did you hear about the guy who knew how to spell bananas, he just didn't know when to stop? I am presently reading the 'Hounds of Spring' By A. C. Swinburne, and when after reading several stanzas aloud to the roar outside this door there was a deafening response, I knew that here is some good stuff. Cordially, Algernon Boosinger."

January 1: "There are no new years. Ponder that. Why in this factory of energy is the floor so cold? I'm sitting here writing this, wearing my only plaid scarf . . . what's going on? Actually because of my perpetual optimistic outlook: seeing the world through rose-colored eye whites (because of staying up all night all year), and because of the beautiful ephemeral (look that one up!) young lady alluded to elsewhere in this ten-ton text (see Sept. 9, last), I do believe there are new years. But don't jump to conclusions; they don't start now on some dismal January first with the floor so cold I have to wear my shoes, oh no, they start every time love strikes. You know, nickels and diamonds, hearts and flour. Is that more or less often than every 365 days? By the way, the computer complex shows all systems go. Where was I? Oh yes, happy new year everybody. Graveyard shift recommends for your new year's reading: Emerson, all of his essays. Cordially, Ralph Waldo Boosinger.

PS: Please do not seize and drink any more of my bottles of Right Knight ginger ale from the communal fridge. I am not interested in the various coinage left in the drawer down there. I cannot drink it and it soothes me not."

September 9: "Dear Log: Keeping it clean in Muscatine here. Don't rush around wishing me wild congratulations, raining gifts on my head, shaking my fevered hand just because I, tonight, as the first leaf of autumn gave up what photosynthetic ghost it had and fell quietly on my head, became engaged (I'm engaged!); it is enough that sometime in a future so distant from these rattling boilers as to be impeccably silent, ah sweet sweet silence, perfect things are going to transpire. No kidding! How can I continue not singing 'CooCoorah-cha!'? How can this computer not blink in astonishment? Because all is well at the power plant, and I (watch out!), am at the helm. Toast: To Roses and graveyards! Cordially, Amory Boosinger."

I stopped reading the stuff then as the room filled with rich steam, and I unplugged the wrecked coffee-pot. Those old entries in the log always left me in an inspired state of embarrassment, remorse, and hope. I had a cup of scalding coffee, and out into the boilers' auditorium for fresh air where I bellowed the last part of Lincoln's second inaugural. After three more cups of coffee, the first part of the post-croquet crapulence cure, I went down to the fridge, precisely to the vegetable drawer which had come to be known as my ginger ale cellar, and retrieved two bottles of Right Knight, the cheapest and most therapeutic ginger ale available in the NATO nations. It is all carbonation. I sat down in the office chair, opened a well-worn book to "Babylon Revisited" and sipped. By the time the lost Charlie Wales felt the poignancy of remorse descend again about locking his wife out in the snow and losing Honoria, his daughter, the serrated edge of Right Knight's bubbletry had cut away a good portion of my hangover. I finished the story and heaved as always a huge sigh. I stood up and stretched. The cure was almost complete. Sweet ginger ale, a balm, a nectar, a salve, in an unsalvaged world. The mountains now were rising in the east, and a bit of salmon light edged their crests.

4

My mother used to say, "Well there buddy, you've got another brand-new day. What are you going to do, blow it?" And I never see the dawn without thinking of her words. I'd been blowing the days lately. In a while, then, the pink would turn gold and the black-purple facade of the mountains would almost vibrate because of the nearness of the sun, and I would go outside and lean against the warm bricks of the building that faintly hummed from the boilers' work, and I'd talk to the sun. "Just a second there, you unruly fool, I'm making my plans for the day . . ." But it would fly up anyway right into my eyes, as I said to myself, "Now, go ahead, make a plan, yes, for a plan, well . . ." Then I'd get the first adrenalin of the day rising like light through my blood. The birds, once spring started showing any faint interest, went absolutely wild during these sunrise moments.

Proctor, keeper of the morning shift, arrived at seven, and I got in my pickup and drove home.

Driving has always, for me, erased things. Thoughts blur like the view out the side window, and are soon, don't you know, far behind. When I arrived home, for a moment I was fresh and untroubled, then some of my latter day confusions caught up. The bigger the problem the faster it arrived. Like a horny toad turned into a dinosaur by the vile radiation of my thinking, these problems were difficult to ditch. The larger ones, as I said, were never far behind; they took monstrous steps. It seemed that there in the fresh blue-grey light of dawn some of them had beat me home, perhaps because the first thing I saw when I got out of the truck once again was the orange croquet mallet in the back. I picked it up and pressed the flat mallet end to my forehead as Godzilla, the scaled question mark, pushed over buildings in my mind looking for a place to park: What, in the most mammoth sense of the interrogative, am I going to do? All I could gather together was the image of Raymond Burr on that island pointing at a crater, saying, "Look at the size of that footprint!"

Upstairs I found Eldon asleep, his helmeted-self slumped over like the last motorcyclist, one hand on the handlebar of the carriage return. He was wearing one of my shirts. I went to the fridge as ritual more than anything else, as inside there was still only a jar of Houbigant Mustard, a six pack of Rocky Mountain Beer, and the hammer that we used to defrost. Well there buddy you've got another brand-new day . . . I selected a beer and went back into the front room and sat down. Outside the birds were impersonating insanity or immortality, one of those significances, by singing a simultaneous medley of the history of all music. It would be hard to die on such a morning, I thought. In the other room I could hear the refrigerator coming in for a landing. I sipped and looked at the Rocky Mountain label: a lumberjack sitting on a log, smiling in those mountains, listening to the birds. He's on drugs, I thought. Rocky Mountain will always be the worst, most tin-can-chemical beer in this solar system.

My watch, the cockeyed precision, dragging me around four hours ahead of time announced: noon. I had a class at 8:50; less than an hour away Banks waited for me in 209 Yates Hall. What would be his choice of weapons? Would he slap me with his handball glove?

I took another drink of the liquid alkali, and put my feet up on the coffee table. Across the room, my disabled American veteran roommate, the only genius besides Riddel I'd ever known, slept on the last page of his book. He'd been maniacally writing the book about his experiences in Viet Nam. Two publishers already wanted it, but they were not in his plans. He said he was only writing it to get all of that shit out of his goddamned way so he could start writing what he called simple expressions of warm enthusiasm for regional magazines, like *Connecticut Yankee* and *Arizona Highways*. He had a convicted disdain for book publishers and academic types. "They'd publish anything, and if it depressed people and made them sick so that they had to run in circles puking, good, as long as the money rolls in. Well, not my sickening book, they won't!" He had nearly been killed in Saigon. He had been an apprentice mechanic; and one day while he was loading a B-52 with bombs, a crane pulley snapped, one fat metal bomb swung out of the hold gently, and touched Eldon upon the forehead like a magician's wand. That's not what he had written about, but he had told me it all in pieces over the year we'd shared our apartment. He had been in a coma for seven months and three operations. He awoke during the fourth to hear someone say they'd taken a cup of blood out of his brain. Then, left unable to talk he had had to relearn the whole messy thing. Now he received fourteen dollars every month and wrote his book, wearing the red football helmet most of the time because half of his skull was gone. I had felt his scalp where only skin lined each magic thought he had. Soft.

Robinson-Duff stirred from his hunchback dreams. He sat up, stretching, delicately withdrew his glasses from his face in the helmet, and rubbed his eyes. "What time is it?"

"Twelve-twenty."

"Less grief, what time?"

"Eight-twenty."

"Good. Do you remember about the film?"

"Yeah, I still have to pick it and the projector up."

"Well I told Ribbo and his pals, so we should have a nice crowd."

"Did you tell them a dollar this time?"

"Yeah, they seemed to think it was okay. Is Lenore coming?"

"I don't know." I held up the beer. "Want a beer?"

"You could tell her she can bring druggy."

"Gary, the pharmacist. No that's not a good idea." These thoughts are piling up, it seemed to me.

He got up and went for the bedroom, pulling off the red hat carefully. His head looked pale, delicate.

"You get off work tonight?" he asked, rubbing his head.

"Yes, Proctor's son is filling in."

"Good, but try and be back early will you, my sister, Evelyn is coming up from Nephi with her son. I want you to meet them."

"Right. I will."

"Well, don't you have a class now or something?" Eldon said. He went into the bedroom.

"We'll see," I hollered, leaving, "Be sure to put up the movies sign!" As I crossed the front lawn, Eldon yelled down from the bedroom window: "Watch out for Mrs. Ellis. She's prowling around with her cowboy son-in-law for the rent. I told her we'd have it tomorrow and she said she didn't like it and was going to see you—since you 'work.' "

"Wonderful."

Mrs. Ellis, our landlady who lived one house down from ours, was sitting on the back bumper of my truck, while her son-in-law, one foot up on the fender, noted my license number. Approaching them, I thought there was a good chance I might be in the L'il Abner comic strip.

"Hi, Mrs. Ellis, how are you?"

"Got the license number on your truck, buster," son-in-law said, pushing his cowboy hat back with his thumb as if he'd just done a day's work.

"Been up to see that other one," Mrs. Ellis interrupted. She always called Eldon the other one, because she thought he was strange in the helmet. "And he ain't got it. You got the rent?"

"Why yes, ma'am. I'm on my way now to make a massive withdrawal from my resourceful bank account, but I have some other errands to run so why don't I bring it over tomorrow, bright and early."

"She means, have you got the rent now? I got the license plate of this truck, buddy." Son-in-law, who only made appearances around rent day, always spoke as if he were chewing something.

"Buster, to you big boy." I said. He took a step toward me and I skirted around the corner of the truck snatching the orange mallet in the process.

"Hey! Watch out!" he threatened, and Mrs. Ellis jumped up and started shaking her pointed fingers at me: hissing. For a while it was one of those scenes where every move he made I made the mirror move, keeping the truck squarely between us. I waved the mallet like the man on the tightrope that I was.

"Come on, boy." Mrs. Ellis finally said after all three of us had gone around the truck twice and I had yelled "Tomorrow, bright and early!" six or seven times. She grabbed her son-in-law by the shirt and walked him away a piece before turning, and shaking both hands like six-shooters in my direction rattled, "We're goin' get the law on you no-goods."

As they marched back to their house, I couldn't help myself. "Tomorrow, bright and early!"

"Shut up, you." he screamed back.

"Get yourself a hobby horse you black-hearted malevolency, you twerp!" That brought him back out the door and my way, but again I threw her into gear and backed out the driveway throwing gravel like intended buckshot under my truck in his direction. Why do things take these turns? I hadn't thought a bad thought about Mrs. Ellis in weeks. When we first moved in she had taken a liking to me, and when I paid the rent would invite me in to read her J. Edgar Hoover letters, and ask me questions about "the other one." She had a file full of letters from J. Edgar Hoover and John Philip Sousa. She had been born on the same day in the same year as Mr. Hoover, as she called him, and when she discovered creation's design, she had begun sending him homemade socks every year on their birthdays. He sent her back letters of thanks saying how unique her actions were in a world like this. She knew Sousa from when he was a soda jerk, and always talked as though they had been lovers, but his letters, responses to her praise for his music, sounded awfully formal to me. Anyway I found all that stuff interesting, and never dreamed that this woman, who had even said once she'd make a pair of socks for me, would be relating to me in a law enforcement manner. I knew she was concerned about me and "the other one," because she'd always ask, "What does he do all day up there?" And when I'd say, "Write," she'd snap, "What do you mean?"

Once after towing Eldon's car to a garage, she intercepted me as I carried the rope up to the apartment, and said, "Oh no you don't. Just put that back in your truck."

It was the only rope I had and I didn't want it to get stolen, but she went on, "Three years ago Isson shot himself in that place and it cost me sixty-five dollars to clean the rug. I don't know what you're up to but just leave the rope in the truck." So I expected some things, but never that it would be the form of war we now enacted.

With troubles sitting like illegal migrant workers in the back of the truck, no losing any of them, more getting on at every stop, I drove up to the university. I went to Yates Hall, but there were not many ways I could've entered Banks's class. I stood there listening at the door, and I couldn't go in. It was as unintelligible out there as inside. Poor deformed and misunderstood *Richard III.* Personal appearance plays a role in political and social success, the play tells us. Banks had me. At least our schism was the result of a tangible, real-world occurrence. Splitting over an idea, say whether or not the puns in *Lear* are worth writing about would have been too inconclusive, too abstract. Now, acts had been committed and there was no going back. The difficulty arose from the fact that there was also no going forward. While in diminishing quantities I do believe you can repeat the past, or at least say I do, I knew Banks wasn't going to erase one backseat image from his photographic memory for several lifetimes. One of them mine. So after thirty minutes of standing by that vibrating door, I exited the building having made a permanent decision about Shakespeare's tragedies: I wouldn't be able to study them under Banks. Perhaps I wouldn't study them at all. As I saw it I was walking down the last corridor of the university, but down there just a ways I could see Banks, like any three-headed dog, guarding the gate. I couldn't get out, and the old Godzillian question: What now?

I found my course evaluation card and wrote, "This guy lives what he teaches!!!!" across the front and dropped it into the campus mail on my way, as I saw it, out.

5

This was a period in my life when all hitchhikers seemed to be Dotty Everest. I sometimes think she sat on the curb outside the driveway waiting for me to go somewhere. Oh I had paid her certain attentions, but that had been before I really knew her. We'd met, naturally, in the cafeteria line one Thursday during my Zelda period, which I am reminded is still enduring, and after a brief dialogue about the meatloaf, we spent the remainder of the weekend in Park City mining for gold and throwing smokey wine glasses against handy granite surfaces. I had initially been attracted to her by her plum leotards which she wore, I came to know, absolutely everywhere, trussed in some kind of athletic bra that made artillery shells out of what could have been pleasant breasts. Her ambitions toward dance I found agreeable, not knowing that to her it may as well have been tennis or weightlifting. And she thought it was her duty to be regarded as the "nut" her sorority sisters had named her, so she went around being dutifully zany, yet always, in the end, pulling down straight A's. Is this to say a flirt? I'm not sure. Regardless, there she was again, thumb out, plum leotards and a loose red skirt. She did *look* like a dancer.

"Well, greetings old friend," she said leaping up.

"Hi Dotty."

"Where you going? Don't tell me: uranium mining near Wendover. I'm game."

"I know you are. All right, here we go."

"Still onto 'Adventures?' "

"Mildly."

"Where *are* you going." She said, swinging her bag over onto the seat.

"To do some cinematic research."

"I'm game. I don't have a class until this afternoon."

She sat up cross-legged on the seat, in what couldn't have been a comfortable position, but that was all right because it was all to show the proper disregard for her skirt, an openness that she assumed dancers all shared.

"How's old age?" This is the way she referred to my being engaged.

"Like everything else."

"Anything I can do?"

"N-O."

When we got to Higgins Film Co., she hopped out and opened the door for me, saying as we went in, "Easy there old fella, you really oughta get a checkup, you know, arteries, heart, things like that."

Old Higgins was sitting at his desk sorting scraps of film into Mason jars, smiling as he stared up through each strip.

"Hello, Mr. Higgins." I'd rented films from him before.

"Ah," he said turning, "hello." He'd recognized his name, not me.

"I'd like to rent a science-fiction film like before, remember, when I got, *It Came from Beneath the Sea.*"

"Ah. Yes." He stood out of his wooden swivel chair. He was always shorter than I expected. "Now, would you like an Earth Monster or an Alien Visitor type film?" He rubbed his pale hands together.

"Well, I don't know, but I think," I looked at Dotty, "I'd like an Alien Visitor type film."

"Hmmm. An Alien Visitor film . . ." His eyes narrowed in thought, and he led us into the back. Dotty followed close, rubbing what breast she could against my arms. A dark row of closets lined the back room, and in the dark, dust filtered down off of the first copies of *Intolerance.* Mr. Higgins opened a closet with a creak and a groan, one from the closet, the other from him, and a dust-coated film can rolled out and around the floor like a coin. He ignored it, peering deeper into the crypt. I couldn't see a thing.

"Ahh, hmm." He said stretching the exploratory humming into a minute. "Ah. Hah." And he jumped back as a rumble started in the closet, and he quickly handed me a reel, then two others. We could still hear things falling down back there as we stood in the front office and he blew balloons of dust off the three reels. Mr. Higgins wrote a receipt on the back of an old grocery list on his desk, saying, "This, my boy, is a great film."

"What is it?"

"Twenty Million Miles from Earth."

In the truck, Dotty held the reels up to her like schoolbooks, showing either a great love for the cinema or no fear of getting dirty.

"Sounds like a good film. What time is the showing?"

"Eight."

"I'm game."

I let her off in front of Sorenson, the stately old administration building, whose upper floors were dance and yoga studios. Arcs of dust reached across the purple crescents of her unsubtle artillery, and in a scene designed to send Archimedes into the arms of Freud, she stood there a moment brushing herself off, liberally. "Later," she said slamming the door and running up the hundred marble steps.

Oliver Grinmaster's most salient characteristic was his unending mercantile irony. For instance, he named the ancient white brick market he owns and runs, "The Taj Mahal Food Center." He really hadn't done it jokingly. When his wife came back from the tour he'd sent her on with the university, he'd had an epiphany one evening in their den looking at the slides. He told me he looked at the Taj Mahal for two hours after his wife had gone to bed, burning the projector light up, melting the slide, and scorching the veneer on the coffee table in the heat of his vision. The next morning he had pulled down the neon-lettered PALACE GROCERIES sign and ordered the new revolving electric dome that sat upon his empire even now. Eldon and I owed the Taj Mahal forty bucks from its "Palace Grocery" days, and going in there was always some kind of trial. I threw three cases of Coors up on the counter.

"Morning, sahib." He liked me to call him that.

"Why Boosinger, it's you. Purchasing some items from the Taj Mahal."

"Seems to be."

"Don't you want to charge it?" The huge hand-lettered cardboard mobile spelling out NO CREDIT swung back and forth above his head.

"Sure put it on the account." I handed him the exact change for the beer.

"Fine, Fine. You know, you guys can pay me any day now if you'd care to. I mean not that I want to pay any of my own bills with the money you've been holding out on me, I just would like to see things that I don't think really exist."

"Yeah. Well we're getting the money together now. We should be clearing it all up at any minute."

"In the meantime," he said leaning over the beer, "are you sure you need all this?"

"You're right, I might need some more. Got any?" I looked back toward the cooler.

"Just a minute, there, my dear debtor, if you've got coins for beer, you got coins for past debts."

"No way, Mr. Grinmaster, we're entertaining some important dignitaries tonight."

"Oh, why didn't you say so? That's entirely different." He didn't move off the beer.

"I'll say it is," I growled, jerking the three cases out from under his pointed elbows, heading out. "They're from India visiting, hoping to sue this weevil pit for libel!"

I fell over a sandwich sign announcing a new low on cat food on my way back to the truck, but reached it and tossed the beer in the back. He came out the door of the Taj Mahal and, rubbing his nervous hands in his apron, said, "If I'm dead by the time you pay that bill, Boossinger, just donate it to a fund for rehabilitating the young idiots who are dragging this country down, will you!" See what I mean about irony. Regardless, I kept on going there because it was several billion times better than Seven-Eleven. I like Grinmaster, and, in a way, the attention he pays to me.

The sunrise adrenalin now started to ebb, and I was on my

own for the last errand. Fortunately it lay in sympathetic territory: the dormitory office. Christine, my thirty-year-old, one-time typist, and assistant dean of housing was in.

"Larry! Great to see you. Back prowling the old home turf? How's your lady?' "

"Perfect," I said. Everybody called Lenore "the lady."

"How are you?"

"Imperfect. That is the same, but that's immaterial. I have come to invite you to a film that could change your life."

"What? You mean it would make Rolly propose?"

"No. I mean change your life for the better. Forget that freak. But you can invite him too if he pays his own way."

"What is it this time?"

"*Twenty Million Miles from Earth.*"

"Huh?"

"An informative intergalactic travelogue."

"Well," she said, clasping her hands behind her head, sitting back, hoisting her pendulous twin mammalian timekeepers, "the projector is in the same cupboard as when you were here." She pointed. "How's the degree coming? Got any papers for me to type?"

"A wrong question."

"Sorry. Listen, I'll try and make it." She prepared to go back to her paperwork.

"Good." I gripped the projector.

"Oh, Larry," she said, going for her desk drawer as if it was a holster, pulling out a loaded folder, "your final bills came, for the last two months and cleaning."

6

At home I avoided all the Ellises and found the little yellow sign outside our apartment door that said: "Movies Tonite, Yippie!!" in Eldon's elementary school script. Inside he was rigging the cord onto our tapestry, so that when he pulled on it, the whole thing rolled up revealing the bare wall: our screen. A showman's touch. The tapestry was predominantly of snorting horses and the huntsmen they carried, and way back on a hill in the green and sepia distance, was a little red fox. The huntsmen were looking the wrong way as their spotted dogs went berserk at the horses' feet.

"Get everything?"

"Everything. Grinmaster sends his best wishes."

"I'll bet."

"Want a beer?"

"Sure." We sat down on the couch looking out at the traffic. "Who's coming?" I asked.

"I'm not sure. Some of the Student Political Alliance people, and their candidate—Harmon, I think. Ribbo and the freaks. A Black Heron contingent. Assorted females."

"Sordid?"

"Probably, who'd you invite?"

"Wesson. Virgil Benson. I think Dotty Everest is coming."

"Why'd you ask Wesson and Everest?"

"Why do people do things in this world?"

"Is Lenore coming?"

"I don't know." My instinctual phrase.

"Well it sounds like a great party, I just hope we raise some money. I'll have to do my DAV Speech, number four. The one about some people having advantages others don't."

We moved the furniture into the small bedroom, stacking the couch and the overstuffed on the bed, knocking the phone over as usual. We decided to leave the desk this time and put the projector on it instead of in the bathroom as we had in the past. Putting the projector back in the bathroom gave us a larger picture, but also forty thousand intermissions. There was a knock on the door.

"Evelyn! Come in." A woman came into the room looking more like Jean Arthur than I could believe. "Evelyn, this is Larry; Larry, my sister Evelyn. And this is Zeke." I shook hands with the dark-haired boy. He was three or four, and really liked shaking hands.

"Glad to make your acquaintance, I'm sure." he said.

"Gosh, Eldon, don't you boys have any furniture?"

We all sat on the floor and I got two more beers and a glass of wine for Eldon's sister. She had taken the bus from Nephi that morning and she and Zeke told us the wonders of central Utah, until darkness closed in on the orange end of Eldon's cigarette.

Then I set up the projector and the first reel, and people started arriving. Dotty arrived first, of course, towing some "Sandy," the best male dancer in the company. Then Simpson and his new bride. Wesson, who helpfully gave Virgil Benson a ride. Most of the Student Political Alliance looking serious and talked out, pamphlets hanging from their back pockets like tails. Edith, and Jannie, and Sharon, all friends of Eldon's. A whole crowd of sophomore "chicks," which in this case is the right, most charitable word for them. I think one of them was a cheerleader. Two hard-looking Black Heron regulars, one already drunk. Johnny Harmon, candidate for student body president in tomorrow's election, along with two groupies. Every time the door opened my heart yawned, in Lenore expectation. Eldon handed out drinks for a while and kept Wesson away from me. I knew Wesson was just churning to know what I'd done to give Banks such a negative coronary thrill, and then chime in with too-late warnings and codes of conduct for the future. Then Eldon made a very brief and moving fundraising speech, during which he removed his glasses twice, emphasizing the word "privileges." His helmet, as I have indicated earlier, was awesome. He then pulled the cord raising the eternally frustrated fox hunters in a roll, as I turned on the switch and a black and white *Scrappy* cartoon danced on the wall.

As soon as the cartoon was over, I left my post and helped Evelyn put Zeke to bed across the hall in our neighbor, Bunny's apartment. Bunny, an entertainer in a way herself, always came to our parties and left her apartment open as a measure of convenience.

"You have some interesting friends." Evelyn said pulling the sheet up to Zeke's chin.

"Wherever they may be." I shouldn't have said.

"What?"

"Nothing. Goodnight, Old Zeke."

"Goodnight, Old Larry."

Back at the theater, the rocket carrying the Alien Visitor had just arrived on earth from twenty million miles in outer space, and Dotty came over and edged between Evelyn and myself.

"Really a great film."

"Cease perturbing the projectionist please."

"Old man."

She rejoined Sandy. Eldon sat on the window sill with Jannie, whispering occasionally, his helmet reflecting the antic light from the wall, the trees behind him growing quietly greener. Outside, lilacs.

After the Italian boy took the capsule home to amaze his father, a tremendous shadow appeared on the screen. Simpson and his bride, she rising first, stood up and exchanged one too many edged words while silhouetted in the small Italian house trailer where the Alien Visitor would grow up. Stepping over bodies, they left. Marriage. This science-fiction must be strong stuff. Simpson had once been a famous friend of ours.

Ribbo and the freaks arrived stoned. He handed me the joint as he came in saying, "Where's Simpson going?"

"Home."

"Far out. He said the movie is about a lizard, is that right?"

"That lizard," I pointed out of the projection booth, which I wore like a mask, at the Alien Visitor.

"Wow!" he noted in a breath and headed for the kitchen.

The relatively scaly Alien Visitor, reminiscent of the creature of the black lagoon from the film of the same name (though the special effects in *Twenty Million Miles* are much better) was now being scrutinized as he went through many Disneyesque, that is to say anthropomorphic, movements, in a small glass case. And the reel clack-clacked to a close.

Everybody rose and went into the kitchen to get another drink, or to the bathroom. Some people strolled across to Bunny's. I saw Ribbo go up and assure Johnny Harmon that he had the freak vote. Everyone assumed Ribbo had extensive influence that way, because he had an enormous underground comic collection, which he kept on his pad's cubic version of a coffee table just like Professor Roachfield keeps *Overview* on his. Whenever Ribbo got into a situation where he felt his power waning, he would begin muttering, "Guns, money, men, guns, money, men, . . ." Harmon was moving freely through the crowd. Fortunately there were no babies for him to kiss. Then he talked to Edith and Sharon for a while. Smiling at him, they sat Indian-style on the floor, nodding, as he tried to organize their bloc. The three of them made an attractive picture; and he appeared magnetic, larger than life. As I snapped down the last projector facet and readied reel two, Eldon looked over to me, "Is she coming?" I don't know what's going to happen. Am I uncommitted? How can I gain a little magnetism? Even a little static electricity? How do people get larger than life?

A "Bullshit!" or two came from the audience as the Alien Visitor suddenly sprouted man-size, and committed the first overt act of rural violence. For a minute the beer-traffic in the room slowed as people received their dollar's worth from the film.

A thin line of light from the door projected Evelyn's shadow as she returned from Bunny's where she'd been checking on sleepy Zeke. Smoke rose through the projector beam in occasional streams, and Evelyn smiled to see the closeup of the Alien Visitor's profile: like Abe Lincoln with scales.

"He's asleep." she whispered to me.

"Good."

"What a peculiar film."

"Yeah isn't it great? Want some more wine?"

"No, I'll wait."

"Here, Evelyn, sit here in the booth." I cleared a little place for her on the edge of the desk. As she sat down, some of my books fell off the other side. One weighs some things against others, I suppose.

Fish-man from outer space had grown to his fully spurned fifty feet and made huge strides toward Rome, as all young upcomers in Italy should. There was a shot of the hustle and bustle of downtown Rome with the many citizens going about their daily business in the real world. It became pretty obvious by now, as members of the audience passed the ninth round of beer among themselves, that the Alien Visitor was not going to make it; this is just not his world. All the moviegoers' hair reflected the blinking grey light from the screen, as the projector, oversize in the crowded room, whirred and sputtered, in a small continuous fit of heat and light.

It was at that moment when Lenore stepped into the plank of hall light from the doorway and took a hold of my elbow. Firmly. Behind her in the hall was friend Gary, the pharmacist. They were overdressed, Gary wearing a sealskin overcoat for some reason, and I saw, not staying. Lenore, looking more at my hand than at me and still holding my elbow, pressed the ring down into the flesh of my palm as if she were putting out a cigarette and Smokey the Bear was watching. They walked to the stairwell and turned. "Think it over, Larry," was all she said, leaving. Probably for Rome.

What could I have said? I actually mean this, what could I have said? Ouch? She had looked perfect in a lime-colored dress, light as air, under which as perfection allows there must have been lime underwear. I confess a sublime ignorance of what is supposed to be done. Would I go then years from that night to her front door only to be invited in and expected to ask questions about her babies? How's little Gary, Jr.?

Turning back into the room I saw that Eldon had witnessed this little exchange, and he turned his back on the film and sat with his feet on the roof. I shut the door and walked carefully over to Bunny's, fell on the sofa and lit a cigarette from her plexiglass cigarette box. The initials K.B.L. were cut nicely in the top. Superman once compressed a piece of coal in his bare hand into a diamond to impress a witchdoctor after Jimmy and

Lois's plane had crashed. I rolled the perfect gem between my thumb and first finger, feeling the corners. I thee wed. I threw my feet up on the table and blew three malformed smoke rings at the ceiling. Bunny's terrace doors were open and the breeze erased the rings, bringing in a large dosage of lilacs. Evidently they had the house surrounded. Trying to pause, to gather, I tried to calculate how many hours I had been awake. My mouth tasted tannic and my closed eyes felt slack. "Oh la." went the sigh.

After several long minutes that seemed an interminable exhalation, I heard the general shuffle that told me: end reel two. Ribbo strolled in accompanying one of the nubile cheerleaders. She was fairly drunk, and he was doing his people's logic voice into her incoherent face, all the while keeping his underground arm around her waist, "I don't do football games, because the sanctified violence is absurd. Fans aren't the people. The people can't afford to do football games, they're stuck in the streets . . ." They went out onto the terrace. Ribbo used the verb "do" for everything. He was going to do some dope. He was going to do some sleep. He was going to do the revolution. That verbal umbrella didn't bother me as much as going to the salmonella cellar he lived in; I mean, he never did the dishes.

In our kitchen the empties overflowed the garbage sack. Somebody had started a trend by putting his cigarette out in the sink.

"How's the beer?" I asked Eldon.

"Holding out. How are you?"

"Holding out. On with the show, I guess." I stepped back over the people and debris, Dotty playfully grabbed my foot and I nearly fell onto Wesson and Virgil Benson.

"Dotty!"

"Yeah, graceful?"

Never mind, Dotty.

Wesson had been feigning an interest in the film for an hour and a half, and he looked wasted, shell-shocked. He'd been trying too hard to figure out what disorder would cause people to watch such a movie.

"Really superb." Virgil said smiling. I sat down by him a minute. "The animation is amazing. I've seen photos of that model; it's only two feet tall."

"Two feet!" Wesson was astounded.

"Right. And did you notice how expertly he uses his tail? They really knew what they were doing. I think a guy named Harryhausen did it." Benson's collection of *Famous Monsters of Filmland* was much more extensive than my own. "I can't wait to see this finale, I've heard about it."

I started reel three. The dramatic countdown: 10 X 9 X 8 XX blank 4 X, then that slick numberless black flickering. My instincts were not communicating how I should feel. My pockets were full of diamonds, remember. The Italian Army, a fully equipped modern-type army, had been called in. The phone rang. Men with walkie talkies directed traffic.

"Larry here." I always answer the phone like that; I find it reassuring.

"Who's up there?" Accusingly said.

"Eldon and I and a friend."

"What's that noise?"

"The army versus the monster."

"What?"

"Nothing. I don't know what you can hear. We're just sitting around up here looking at the walls, Mrs. Ellis." As I said her name, Eldon tossed another beer can out over the roof onto the lawn.

"Well, why are you in the kitchen?"

"Making sandwiches, ma'am."

"At eleven-thirty?"

"Yes, ma'am."

"Well can't you use someone else's kitchen?"

"No, ma'am."

"Well, I don't like it."

"I'm bringing the rent over bright and . . ."

She hung up. Tanks rolled in and troop convoys converged.

"He's heading for the circus!" the commander, who looked like Gene Barry, said. The now fully misunderstood monster turned left, eyes searching, turned right, looking frantically for the way to go. An elephant looked up from his straw dinner. This unmistakable montage was accompanied by the ringing of the phone. Eldon answered and experienced one of the shortest conversations on record. He waved to me and I shut down the projector.

"That was Mrs. Ellis, our cinephobic landlady. She says she's called the police. I hate to tell you all this, since this last reel, I've been informed, is a prize winner, and we're continuing regardless of the consequences, which is the manner in which we do most things. Leave at your own risk! It may be only a threat since she calls us nightly and says the same thing."

Wesson and Johnny Harmon were the first to leave, and then nearly everyone left. Even Dotty. Being zany is good; jail is bad. Bunny and Virgil Benson stayed. Bunny said she was curious which officer would arrive, and Benson simply said he couldn't miss the ending. Eldon and Evelyn stayed, Evelyn asking if we thought a policeman would really come. I woke one of the Black Heron regulars, a former creative writing teacher in whose irrigated brain nothing more would grow, who was sleeping in the desk well, and he left, muttering about an absolutely frightening dream.

The place was a wreck. It looked like the day after The Little Big Horn. But it was a comfortable wreck, and we all stretched out amid the beer can rubble, spilled wine, and cigarette butts. Art for our sake.

Eldon leaned over toward me and asked, "What did she say?"

"She said think it over." I handed him the ring.

"Think it over?"

"Yeah."

"What did you say?"

"I said, 'Ouch!' "

"Sweet Lord." He sighed. "What are you going to do?"

"Watch the movie. I hate these intimate interviews."

" 'Ouch?' You need help."

"Not yours. Not now."

The elephant had a good grip on the Alien Visitor's right arm as they wrestled outside the huge circus tent, and he nearly flipped the monster onto his head. Ribbo came bursting back in.

"The pigs here yet?"

"No. Sit down and watch the movie."

"They can't invade your private abode without a search warrant."

"Shhh, Ribbo." I pointed at the screen.

The Alien Visitor circled the elephant in a crouch like the one Krusher Kowalski does, head down, arms out. He slapped a double hammer-lock on the screaming pachyderm, and quickly flopped the beast over on its side. Cleverly for this part I turned the volume up full blast: Raahhrrr! Eeeeaaahhh! Rreeaarrk! Rak!

Knock Knock. Our neighbors in the next apartment, a young engineering student from Thailand and his wife, came over to see if our pets were okay. We didn't have any, so they were fine.

"Sure, please come in." They chose to share a beer and sat on the floor, happy to be at the movies. Fire and advance became the army's tactic. Volley after irritating volley drove the Alien Visitor, no kidding, up the Colosseum. The ending of the film is a parallel with *King Kong,* except beauty doesn't kill the beast, just an inability to understand his environment. And vice versa.

At this point, obviously gone crazy in his booth, the projectionist turned the projector out so the beam shot under the open window, across the yard and the film image fell blinking against the leafy texture of the tree. It then looked more like the impressionistic film that it was. Everyone's heads followed the film, and we all climbed out onto the roof for the ending.

"This is funny," Evelyn said. "I've never seen a movie this way before."

The Alien Visitor appealed heavenward a moment, leaning on his tail, arms flailing, face looking for an answer. Is there help anywhere? Finally a particularly salient volley knocked the amphibian Alien Visitor back where he missed a step, and he fell like the last gladiator onto his scaly head on the pavement.

"Oh no!" Eldon spoke for all of us, and lofted his beer can through the beam, as we all did, the cans landing with a soft tink on the front yard. Of course then we heard the sirens, and the police car pulled up in front under the tree as the last closeup tableau of the jeeps and the monster and the commander sighing his grim relief showed on the tree.

"What are you doing up there?"

"Watching the tree."

That brought him right up the stairs just as our Thailand neighbors ducked next door. I forced Virgil Benson to go with them. The policeman took one look around and decided to take us downtown.

"Why Ward Sawyer, how nice to see you again." Bunny smiled.

"Miss Lancaster! Why are you here?" The policeman took his hat off. "You're not disturbing the peace with these punks. Why don't you just slip home."

"Watch your language, Pig!" Ribbo had to say. The cop came forward, toward Ribbo, putting his hat back on, but Bunny interceded.

"I know it's not my usual, Officer Sawyer," she said, "But, yes I guess I was disturbing as much of the peace as these boys."

"Disturbing the peace!" Ribbo said, "There is no peace!"

"Look, you. Your mouth is in for trouble."

"Yeah?"

"Look," I said, "Officer Sawyer, could we just set the customary wheels of justice in motion and proceed?" Then to Ribbo, "Cease this petty harassment of our law enforcement officials." He glared at me. "Or I'll do your nose. Save the revolution for something a little more meaty than this cinematic infraction."

"Sell-out."

We all went downtown. Bunny insisted on coming. After leveling a twenty–five-dollar fine against the projectionist, and delivering a warning lecture that reminded me of the way Wesson talks to me, Officer Sawyer released us to our own recognizance, our own custody, which I thought was a fairly amazing thing to do. "Gee, I hope I don't do anything wrong, I'm in my own custody."

Thinking Eldon was a smartass freak, Sawyer had made him remove the helmet, and on the way back down the stairs Eldon put it back on and grabbed himself sternly by the bicep, saying, "This way Robinson-Duff. Don't get any ideas!" I had myself by the back of the collar and walked along in pain, in custody. Evelyn followed, laughing.

"That wasn't too bad, was it, Ribbo?" Bunny asked him.

"We still should've got to do a lawyer."

"I've never been in jail before." Evelyn said.

"Say do you folks want to do breakfast at my house?"

"I don't think so Ribbo. It's a bit early. How are the dishes?"

"I threw them out. I'm doing recycled paper plates now."

"Thanks just the same."

"Right, well I gotta go then and help with the election. See you later."

"Best of luck."

"Yeah, well it doesn't really matter. If the system doesn't work, there are alternatives you know." He walked off in a stride very like people who are attempting to continue trucking.

7

My watch said six-thirty. We went back to the apartment, walking up the stairs through the filmic debris. Empty, the room looked awful, mainly cans and ashes. The worst detail was a purple-red stain growing on the carpet outward from the kitchen. I found an overturned gallon jug of Paisano.

"Yeech!"

"Make some coffee, will you Larry?" Eldon said, carrying the chairs back out of the bedroom.

"Sure." This is when I reached in the fridge, found an opened, but cold can of coke and took a huge slug, hoping to alleviate the furnace all the beer was making out of my body. There was a cigarette butt in it; I puked into the sink. There are times when I rejoice that I am not my body. After several antiseptic, hot-water minutes I had the kitchen sparkling, and the coffee pot gurgled in my little version of order. I felt better, but I knew there were things unpurged.

"What are you doing in there?"

"Cleaning up. Coffee will be ready in a minute."

Evelyn went next door and retrieved Zeke, who then slept on our bed. Bunny came back over and handed me a bottle of ginger ale; it wasn't Right Knight, but it was exactly what I needed.

Then the four of us sat in the littered front room, as if we were bemused about the hopeless state of domestic help, and tried to sip our steaming coffee. Eldon removed his helmet and his fragile wire glasses and rubbed his eyes. I was always afraid he was going to rub too hard. He told us a little about his book, about one extended metaphor where he compared the Vietnamese with American Indians, but he wouldn't really go beyond that because, "It's too depressing." I told them about my story idea about the rest home. They seemed to like it. Then Evelyn told a very simple reverential story about her husband and how he was killed at a lumber plant in Fredonia, just south of Kanab. He'd been buried in sawdust when a chute broke open. She didn't say much about it, but the way she talked was beautiful.

"Why don't you have a girl?" she asked me.

"He does, Evelyn."

"You do! What's her name?"

"Lenore." Eldon seemed to be answering for me.

"That's a lovely name. Are you two serious?"

"He's only serious about Scott Fitzgerald." Eldon pointed to the portrait of Fitzgerald I keep on the wall. "They're engaged."

"Ignore him." I said. "We *were* serious."

"Oh, you ought to get married."

"You think so?"

"Sure!" Eldon interrupted, "Scott is dead; Lenore has walked out: that leaves Dotty."

"Dotty?" Evelyn asked.

"Dry up, Robinson-Duff."

"You see, Evelyn, Larry here is a romantic. He's *very, very* different from you or I. Why I might marry an intelligent, beautiful lady (who I might add is in med school), if we were in love. Yes I might. That just shows how stupid, insensitive, and unromantic I am. Larry, here, the romantic on the other hand, prefers instead to marry his dream. You see, he's . . . ."

"Robinson-Duff sometimes you talk just like the disabled American Veteran that you are. Perhaps you should replace the helmet, in case I begin hurling my books once again."

We heard crying in the other room. Zeke woke from a nightmare. While Evelyn was in the bedroom comforting him, the three of us sat in silence. When she returned we all settled further, realizing we'd broken the night's back and each minute now was ascension toward morning. Bunny smoked Salems, a mentholated product I learned to dislike later in another country, but I had one that night too, as if to foreshadow the smoldering months to come. Eldon, then, left me alone, and started talking about things he'd never told me before. The entire time he spoke, I was mesmerized by the vision of his soft, tousled head and the coffee vapor on the window.

"I heard them say in echoes, 'a cupful of blood, a cupful,' and when I woke Evelyn was there, swollen to the limit, pregnant."

"With Zeke," Evelyn added. "The first thing he did was point and smile. I think he thought I was in trouble." It became clear that Eldon and Evelyn were having a private conversation, saying things they'd never discussed before, and they needed Bunny and me there so they could pretend it wasn't as important to them as it was, so they could talk this way.

"I did." Eldon said. "Everybody's in trouble; pregnant ladies just have company. Anyway, fat Evelyn made some flash cards with the word on one side, you know, 'Chair,' 'Dog,' and the picture on the other. The artwork was fantastic. Grandma Moses–like. Clear. And she'd flash these goddamned cards at me two hours a day. Dog. Chair. Hand. Eye. Bird. Rain. That was a good card. She had a cloud raining this slanted blue rain onto a little stick figure girl with an umbrella. I thought that card was 'Girl' for the longest time. She'd flash that card and my mind would slip one gear. I mean at the time I could feel my mind slip, click, and I'd dream about walking with that girl. The rain. The smell of the girl's sweater. Coming to her house. The porch." Eldon paused. The four of us didn't look at each other, just out at the long purple-grey dawn.

"It's kind of a trite picture, I know," he said, "But, god, it was real to me . . ." He paused again.

"Yeah. Then cards. Every day. 'Tree.' 'Shovel.' 'Man.' 'Flowers.' Sometimes I could follow, pay attention. But mostly each picture was a trigger for strings of images. I could remember the accident vividly. Arnold yelling 'Heads!' and ducking by the wing, the bomb in its sling swinging back out of the plane, slowly, my only thoughts were that it wasn't supposed to do that and how fast accidents happen, how they change things. I didn't see it hit me. And I'd come back to the cards. 'Car.' 'Boat,' with ridiculous water skiers. 'Plane.' 'Train.' Most of Evelyn's pictures had people in them."

I looked over at Evelyn. She was staring out, and in the slight light she looked ready to cry. I could imagine how desperate she must have been, how much she loved her brother.

"Then it all got better fast. It was like skipping grades. I'd try to talk. I knew the words, and thought I'd say them, just like that, but each time I'd get the mouth open: nothing. Evelyn would stop with the card she had up: 'Mountain.' Her face would get so excited—god! She'd hold it up for me more, closer, pointing to the syllables, saying them for me, turning over to the picture with the snow peak, the tree line, wildflowers, talus, two hikers holding hands, then back to the word itself, but I said nothing. She'd back up a few cards. 'River.' She'd say it. Riv-er. Riv-er. But the mouth hung there slack. It wouldn't work. Then the mouth would shut. God what a strain. We'd both sit back and Evelyn," Eldon interrupted himself here. "Evelyn is it okay that I talk all this, tell all this stuff?"

"Yes, please." She was crying, not moving.

"We'd both sit back breathing and Evelyn would start to cry holding up 'Lake.' 'Fish.' 'Cloud.' 'Hat.' The man in 'Hat' had a wicked mustache, remember Evelyn?" By this time Bunny was crying too.

"Can you see it?" Eldon went on, "She came every day. Two hours. It took five weeks. The thoughts came across my mind first like birds in an alley; I couldn't stop them, any of them, to consider them. Watching some, I'd lose sight of the others. I couldn't grasp them. The mouth would open, but I couldn't get anything out of it.

"Then they became longer and slid in line like tigers and rabbits at a shooting gallery in a penny arcade. One of those machines that uses two mirrors to make them look way way out there. But still for a while, they'd come up and swish, gone before I could nail them. I'd even wait for every third one purposely letting some go by, moving my inner eye.

"Toward the end I could see every one; see the grain of the fur, the cock of the eye itself—until I held them still. 'Cat.' 'Hat.' 'Boat.' 'Coat' . . . 'Mountain.'" He paused. "'Mountain.' I spoke words. Evelyn was the teacher."

"And do you know what word he said first?" Evelyn spoke, still crying a little, from where the first sunslant clipped her face, eyes. She seemed fine.

"Rumpelstiltskin?"

"Pigs. He said 'pigs.' Then 'pigs in the mud.' He took the card from me. It had three pigs in the mud . . ."

"By a white fence." Eldon added.

"By a white fence," Evelyn continued, "And he said 'pigs in the mud.'" Bunny was crying and laughing now, or some combination of those things. "And then he pointed at my stomach and he said, 'trouble.'" Evelyn had stopped crying now, but her eyes and face were all wet so I gave her my handkerchief. We sat a long time letting the sun sweep the room while people wiped their faces.

I was lost myself for a while remembering when I first knew Eldon, and we moved in together and how he was always sleeping, staying in the bedroom because of the skull brace they made him wear. When he was up, he would loiter around the apartment in his pajamas and an old grey sport coat that had been my father's. Then he began the writing, and we began the fishing, and things improved fast.

"Come on." I said at last. "I'll buy you all breakfast. Let's get Zeke up and get out of this wreck."

8

On our way out we met two of the chicks who had left when the military had arrived. "We left our shoes and some things." one explained.

"I put your bra in my bedroom," Bunny said kindly to the other girl who stood arms folded, up way too early in the morning, "Go right in." The girl's mouth quivered slightly.

Everybody climbed into the rear of the truck and I drove us, in a fresh-air frenzy, down to Roberto's, home of the steamy plate-dwarfing onion omelette. Roberto's was crowded with mailmen and bus-drivers, as always, and it was a little too warm in there and I sank into the kind of reverie that has caused others to be put into safe, sanitary places. Things sink in. I started rethinking the big picture. Recent events flew through my head like raining, red-hot asteroids. I was going to review my options, but I couldn't recall seeing them in the first place. Evelyn and Bunny and Eldon, who sat around me talking like the best human beings possible, all had been disconcertingly enthusiastic about my novel idea on the rest home. As I sat there outsized in the big red naughahyde booth, monstrous thoughts strolling freely about my rerinsed mind, trying to discern the definite shape of the waitresses' underthings, an idea I'd had two days previous revisited my mind.

Two mornings before, while driving home from the power plant, I fell behind a stationwagon, two kids in the back. One kid, a blond, crewcut, climbed over the seats until he was right against the back window. When he got there and saw me, the kid raised his chin in a face of unparalleled ugliness and at the same time he flipped the finger at me with both of his nine-year-old hands. At that moment, as at the one I endured at Roberto's, staring at an omelette whose very onion complexion brought tears to the eyes, I decided to leave the country. Drastic measures. Morning of an author.

When we left the restaurant, I selected half an inch of Roberto's postcards, the picture showing a family of four smiling over their Round the World Roberto's Special Omelette Deluxe. I wrote one word of the following sentences on each card: There-are-a-million-loves-in-this-world-but-only-the-right-love-twice.-The-novel-will-be-for-you-Zelda.

I mailed them all to Lenore.

9

A television actor once told me, "Beauty is all in the chin line." Maybe so. But I knew as that day bore on that ugliness must have a good deal to do with eye sockets. Mine were going from light brown to deep grey, my eyes receding all the while. Eldon took Evelyn and Zeke to the bus, while I backed my truck under the window and commenced to clean our apartment. I was really sorry to see her go. She had the largest capacity for hope of any woman I've ever met living in the real world. Even more than Bunny.

At 2:15 when I was sure Banks was in his second class (he teaches like many, the same thing twice; this is known in the department as mileage), teaching the tattered gothic remnants of grotesque Dick III and giving each student an acute awareness of his or her own potential mediocrity, I stole up to school, truck full of junk, and into the teaching associates' office. Susette Bedd, the croquet coquette, was on duty, tweezing her eyebrows. "Hi, how's Banks?" She gave me a very serious "Oh You." look and held the tweezer up like a knife. "Careful, Babe," I said, "one of those beautiful eyebrows is anchored by the brain, you know." I continued over to my desk and started throwing my junk into the fishing creel I'd brought. I cleaned out all the drawers, leaving the lint and paper clips, and then made the mistake of taking down my Lon Chaney poster. This is the sign by which the alert Wesson came to know I was in withdrawal.

"Listen, Honey." I said to the secretary, leaning dangerously close, dropping my phone number on her desk. "When my last two students bring in their papers and leave them on that desk over there," I pointed, "the one that used to be mine, please call me and let me know, okay."

"Cram it."

"I elect not to, dear." I cried, emptying the ashtray into her "Yield" sign coffee cup. "I am a marginal character, and need support and the appropriate phone calls to be kept in check." I cleared a small portion of her desk with my forearm to seal the deal.

When she called two days later a great deal of the drastic measure, all-night confidence had evaporated somehow, I'd paid the rent and slept a little, for instance, but still I had Mexican resolves.

The freshman writing course I had conducted had used the environment as an issue, and the two papers I found on my desk (Susette Chickenheart was out) were: "Junk as Sculpture: Recycling Art" and "Seven Practical Methods Whereby Institutions Could Save Water in Urinals and Toilets". The second paper was accompanied by seven large, startling photographs of toilets with timers, levels, bricks, master switches, and one overhead shot of the bowl and its glistening vortex, mid-flush. Amazing. The renewal of the intellectual brain bank transpires continually.

Also I found a note from Wesson:

> From the Desk of Jeffrey Wesson, Ph.D. Candidate. To: Larry Boosinger: RE: Insanity and permanent mistakes. Message: 1200 noon, Friday. Hub. Tres importante, you fool.

Wesson's desk was across the gang office from mine and was decorated with an oriental tablecloth. A mobile of cardboard eyes hung directly over it, and he had a poster slapped on the ceiling: "Not to choose is to choose," it said straight down at me. I decided not to leave Wesson a message, this being perhaps the last time I'd see him. My watch read a futuristic 4:30, and so I hustled over to the Hub and found Wesson addressing himself vigorously to a baked apple with whipping cream.

"You should have stayed for the last reel the other night."

"Are you kidding? And get arrested and have that on my permanent record, which is where it goes, you know." He stabbed the apple. "Want one of these?"

"No, thanks. What's up Wesson?"

"Listen Lawrence, you're making a mistake."

"Larry, Wesson; and I know it."

"No you don't. Look, you only have a semester and a half to go, and you can cop your degree, which, I might remind you, is eminently more negotiable than this rumored wild-ass scheme to chase Mexican women and write some trivia. I mean it."

"I know, Wesson."

"No you don't, Lawrence, that's why I'm telling you. You Fitzgerald guys are all alike: emotionally unfit to coach girls' softball, ready to reach out for absurdity at any moment."

"Right." Being told I'm like everybody else is one of a dozen ideas, like the concept of snowmobiles, that simply won't go into my head.

"I'm not kidding. Listen to me, Lawrence. I am not kidding. You leave now, and you'll have nothing to sell, nothing in the bank. Look," he calmed down a little, was going to be coldly logical for a moment, "you are bound to failure right now, for these reasons." Wesson held up his hands, intent upon gesturing with his fingers now.

"Thanks, Jeff, this is going to be easier for me to comprehend."

"One, you have no experiences to write about. You are young and stupid." (That last word had trouble getting into my ears.) "Two. You are not Fitzgerald. You will not be him, and you should not chase him. Three. You're a failer, Lawrence, one who fails. I mean it. Wait. Teach. Do research. Why I'll let you help me work on this thing on Chaucer I'm doing."

"Gee, Wesson, really?"

"Sure." Then he saw my face. "Okay, fine, I'd just thought I'd offer some advice. It's your life."

"I'll send you a postcard."

"Don't bother."

10

I turned in the grades for the last two papers, the student who wrote the plumbing paper bringing down a straight A, and I motored south. South, falling out of the bottom of Salt Lake into Provo, Payson, Nephi. In a precedent-setting move I did something that ran contrary to my immediate impulse, and did not stop and see Zeke and Evelyn, but drove on to Richfield. I ate breakfast there at a place that boasted the largest Jim Beam bottle collection in the state. The owner had them lined along shelves near the ceiling. Bottles, permanently cast in ceramic facsimiles of golfers, blue geese, and hunting dogs, celebrated hundreds of centennials. Things go glimmering, Fitzgerald had said. I ate a composite dish known as eggs in the basket, and wondered what they were doing back at the old school.

Driving, as I've implied elsewhere, is inspiration for me, all that stuff whizzing right out of perspective and past your ears, creating change, or the illusion of change, which for me is the same. The sound of the slipping wind in the ill-fitting wing window being the whisper of freedom. The radio broadcast, the stockman's outlook, beef and cattle prices, then Glenna Royanne sang, "Married at the Rodeo," as I swung wide to pass three buxom cowgirls in flowered shirts, their sky blue levis snug in their ponies waving saddles.

Driving hard, I outstripped even the swiftest primeval griefs and I dropped down through the state like a steel ball in a pinball machine, bouncing a few times off the lit bumpers for the bonus score. South on Route 89. Gunnison, Salina, Richfield, Joseph. The Big Rock Candy Mountain, another story entirely, looking like the world's saccharine reserves. I expected to come next to the Valley of Rotten Teeth. South.

Outside of Orderville, a onetime fundamentalist Mormon community, there was a dinosaur skeleton guarding a pile of rocks. On the other side of town a ten-foot stack of deer antlers stood like a massive tumbleweed, intricate as balled haywire. South.

I crossed the muddy Sevier River seven times before seeing the "K" that indicated Kanab. It is said to be the most crooked river in the world, and farmers line the banks with the flattened bodies of old cars to prevent the river from meandering their fields into a series of loopy oxbows. I'd fished the Sevier. It was only good in April, and a person could take some good size Browns, but then the farmers started irrigating and it was all mud and carp. All the good fishing in Utah is high, in the east.

North of Kanab my truck was halted by forty blue-uniformed cavalry as they walked their horses across the road. On the side of a nearby trailer were the words: ED TURNER PRESENTS "THE SUNDOWN BRIGADE"—A TURNER-FOSTER PIC-TURE. The Indians, looking bored, stood by their horses, waiting, in the afternoon.

I passed Fredonia and the mill where Evelyn's husband was killed. The smoke from the immense saw-dust burner drifted across the road, and I ascended into the Kaibab. The broad cut of the Colorado. The Gap. Flagstaff. The RITA H. QUAKENBUSH REALTOR sign. The fifty-foot Paul Bunyan advertising a restaurant. Then the descent from the pines to the desert, to darkness, to the horizontal network of neon that is Phoenix.

I stopped for coffee at a place aside the Black Canyon Highway called "The Roadrunner." The waitress made me eat a fresh chocolate doughnut. I was trying not to be lonely.

The sun came up on the desert the way it must at sea. The

first rays horizontal, only a few mountains around coming straight up surprising themselves in the flatness, looking like battleships armed with cacti. This light glanced the verdant desert first as I raced past Why, Arizona, where I resolved to stop if I ever returned. Permit me, though this isn't a digression, to follow the adamant whips and traces of retrospect and add: I'd be back walking the interrogative streets of Why within a week. Oh facts.

Then I was south of *the* border; I continued the seventy miles to Penasco where I'd been one spring vacation with some guys who knew me in the dorms, that is to say, whoremongers. Penasco smells like salt, shrimp, and diesel exhaust. The shipyards looked like a Brontosaurus skeleton exhibition. I drove out on the cushion of sandy road to the nooked community of Cholla Bay and rented a small house on Pelican Point. It overlooked the ocean, the Gulf of California, a blue-green expanse that extended west to Baja, California, and the ocean came and went at its own will despite the gigantic boulders that sat ominous and smooth as big eggs in front of the house. Stopping my truck like that in another country, I knew it would be at least a few days, possibly weeks until the old raw troubles caught up, and now all I had was writing, one of the finest cottage industries, and one of the finest cottages.

11

Writers' block is not really so much massive cerebral shutdown, as it is a toxic belief in all the bad things people have ever said about you. It is daunting, yes, at points you even want to write letters to all the skeptics in your past congratulating them on their amazing insight, but the gumption, what a fine word, won't even come to write the letters, postcards, let alone get out the stamps and envelopes. So sure, I was struck by a certain amount of this morbid inertia as I sat in front of the typewriter. I thought back to Royal, Wesson, even DeLathaway, that guide. By the time I had left school, I hadn't had much in the bank, emotionally speaking; it wasn't bankruptcy, mind you, simply abject, despondent poverty. At low moments I suspected I heard the transcontinental laughter that Wesson thought he started by ridiculing my writing plans. Lenore filled my head. Gary. What I needed, thinking in Garylike drugstore terms, was relief, even temporary relief. I listened to the tide; I put the coffee on. I think I came to understand why several of my fellow countrymen had turned and fled, in the only avowal they would ever make, to drugs. I listened to the tide. I put the coffee on. I smoked Salems. I straightened my desk, ran to turn off the overboiled coffee.

I started four times in two days, using the breaks to escape to the rocks and fling an assortment of the most unlikely, gaudy steel and plastic lures onto mussel snags, pretending all the time that this actually had some relationship to stream fishing which is a lot to pretend. Stream fishing had made me whole more than once and would again. I hated losing those lures in this gulf. When the tide would go out, I'd rush onto the furthest slick stone and flop about in the foam searching for glimpses of the fluorescent orange gimmicks. I never found a one.

Then the fifth start took, and nine hours later I had a long chapter. It meant more in terms of momentum than storyline. The next day I worked all day, and was feeling so good about our universe and the fatigued exhilaration it offers, that I only got up from the machine occasionally to stride around the room raising my arms and roaring like a lion.

12

The next night Dotty showed up out of a dusty nowhere to punctuate what I still consider to be one of the most important periods in a life.

"How'd you get here?"

"Hitchhiked."

"Why?"

"Rumor is you're not engaged anymore and have reentered life. Do you know they don't speak English down here?"

That is to say, this is when I began acting like a demented tourist (probably a redundancy), worrying about nothing but my suntan and Dotty's suntan line. If we sat three minutes after breakfast, while I drank coffee and contemplated writing, the quick slip into fiction, Dotty became stricken with a virulent form of cabin fever.

"Let's do something," the line went.

"Try the dishes, Dot."

"No. I mean *some*thing."

We did things.

She hated to fish, so we swam and got into what is called serious drinking. We drank tequila until Dotty loved it. I didn't mind it much myself, to be honest, because for the first little while I thought it helped my perspective. My perspective being exactly that of a man on a plane to a strange city who after his second cocktail looks out his first-class window and sees the green and gold grid of South Dakota arcanely cocked at eighty-five degrees. I remembered, as century plant alcohol escorted brain cells out of rooms in my head, Wesson teaching all those freshman comp sections: the Environment, Religious Dilemma, American Metaphor (a class about cars and baseball), and studying Chaucer. Yes, Wesson would make it. He was writing a creative piece, "The Unwritten Canterbury Tales," for Royal. Wesson had even in a clever stroke started spelling Jeff, Geoff, which Royal took as pretty much a divine sign of his student's genius and right to study Chaucer.

During these interludes of self-abuse, Dotty, as far as I could discern, thought of nothing. This isn't fair I know, and sounds vindictive, which at this point, it is. The most intellectual of pursuits she had exhibited, thus far had been spelling words on my back at the beach. She'd describe the letters with her finger, and then say, "Well, what is it?" or "You'll never get it."

"Hamburger."

"How'd you know?"

"Do me a favor from now on, say if you spell cheeseburger, or fries or something."

"What?"

"Stick with all capitals or lower case and no script, all right?"

"Oh all right."

Then I'd spell words on her back: heartburn, malaria, cirrhosis. Her back would go rosy through the tan as my fingers traced the letters.

She got "heartburn" and "cirrhosis" and said, "If you're going to be morbid, I'm going swimming."

I took her into town one day to eat my favorite Mexican dish: Chimi-chongas. It was right after her first day of sun so she covered herself generously with Noxema, and as she walked into the small Sombrero Cafe her smell sent every American tourist in the place back to the first lotion days of his childhood. It was a memorable Noxema moment, the entire place lost in reverie. To this day, the smell of that stuff brings that plum leotard into view, and, worse, I can no longer face the once beautiful fried face of Chimi-chongas.

Nights I could tell when she'd get drunk, because she'd forget the salt with her drink, and every once in a while she'd jam the lemon up to her face and munch on it for several minutes. The nights were hard on her because there was no electricity, and I'd tune in the radio drama from Albuquerque on my transistor, as soon as the sun set. During the day we only got one station from Penasco which we listened to compulsively, memorizing several of the hyperthyroid disc jockey's favorite phrases. I think it unnerved Dotty a bit further that he only spoke Spanish, even the news, and then when it got dark the radio stations came out like stars: Omaha, Denver, Albuquerque, Salt Lake (which I refused to listen to), Phoenix, San Francisco, L.A., and they spoke English into our candle-light (which Dotty described as scary, not romantic), amid the boilerlike rush of the tide.

After the eight o'clock news which was mostly about three families that were kidnapped from Wells, Nevada by two dangerous convicts named Pierce and VanBuren, the radio drama came on and I'd rest my forehead on the tabletop looking at the floor, listening to whatever form the supernatural had taken that night.

Before the first commercial, Dotty would say nervously from her wicker chair, "Let's do something."

After only two days she had an amazingly sharp tan line.

The next evening as I stood again on the farthest wet stone surf casting, Dotty came down from the shanty and stood nearby. I don't think she liked being alone. I was hurling my favorite spinner, a Mepps Sure-fire, the only trinket on which I'd snagged any fish at all, a couple of sand-trout and one small sea bass, and it got snagged. Picture me there, bending my rod backward, in some attempt I guess to haul in the entire bottom of this portion of the Gulf of California, my lips pursed, my eyes a larger conflagration than the reflected setting sun, at the

end of my line. Finally after several back-racking jerks I threw
the pole back on the rocks shattering my reel and entered the
churning sea, following the fish line. My leg brushed against
a rock and I felt the salty bite take flesh. Up to my neck then,
and only feet from where the spinner leeched into the center
of a rock-adhered mussel, I heard Dotty scream: "Larry!
Larry!"

She was pointing at me as far as I could tell. Then thirty feet
beyond me I saw the two fins up and down like the last grey
merry-go-round. Holy Moly. I clambered out stumbling, leaving skin against every rock, emerging in a wash of wet clothes
and stinging weeping lesions. Blood ran down my legs. We
watched the two fins, as if at play, roll by. They might have
been porpoises.

"Dotty," I said snapping the fishline in my teeth, "This is
not going to work."

"Huh?"

"Your being here."

"You don't know how to live."

My kindness extended itself into a vast, border-crossing silence.

13

The next morning we reentered the country, and in a red
sunlight stopped when Why presented itself.

"Why are we stopping?" I got out. She followed. "It doesn't
bother me if you've stopped talking, Mr. Strange."

The woman behind the counter answered, "Yes, this is

Why." as she had ten thousand times before and gave me a postcard. There has got to be a better reason I thought. Dotty bought a fudgesicle.

"You really are strange, mister," she said as she got back in the truck.

At her request I dropped Dotty off in Phoenix with a friend of her brother's. This young friend of her brother's came to the door of his trailer and the most wizened version of deja vu came across his face that I've ever seen.

"Hello, Dorothy," he said softly.

Dotty started to introduce me as playing some part in a fictional romance entitled "The International Affair."

"We were fishing." I explained. "They weren't biting."

Regardless, poor trailer-bound brother's friend receded into a swampy state of mind not distant from my own. He had some stake in Dorothy.

It was when she said, "Larry here is just the neatest writer," that I confirmed my incipient decision to change my life. Dot was pouring it on heavily in the air-conditioned trailer's front room. I kept feeling the transiency of the walls, their flimsiness, one driver berserk on his own lost dreams could erase our little tinlike parlor drama entirely. I hadn't heard her talk so antically before; our Mexican fiasco sounded like a beach party movie staring Richard Burton and Elizabeth, his former spouse, so finally, and probably because of my growing claustrophobic nausea for fiction, I interjected, "No way, Dotty, see you around."

"When you bend over!" she said.

14

I burned off a good deal of the dross of recent encounters, including smugness, irony, and euphoria by listening to Garner Ted Armstrong all the speeding way to Flagstaff, where I stopped and sent Wesson a postcard: "You were right old Geoffrey; it was not to be. All three reasons. Plus fiction sucks. I have resigned myself, and am happy as a bell-hop here in Seattle. Good luck with the Tales. I know you'll do a fine work. Cordially, Larry." The other side of the card showed a man in a red lumberjack shirt being chased up a pine tree by two bears.

15

I continued up through the Navajo reservation's badlands passing all the chromed trucks full of Indians. The government gave them thousands of acres of poisoned sand, not a weed in sight and said, "Do with this what you will. It's yours, really." A person could cast down his bucket a long time in a place like that and get nothing but sparks. Eldon should come down here and write an article; but these landscapes, framed so alkalinely in my windshield would never make the pages of *Arizona Highways*.

At 2:00 A.M. I pulled my old green pickup into the sage ten miles into Utah, near the Coral Pink Sand Dunes, and rolled my sleeping bag out into the back. Lying there looking up at the same billion stars, I decided to shuck my recent affections. I decided to *do* things. Rodeos, perhaps. Western music for sure. Find the rungs of the ladder that lead a person to ride a snorting silver stallion into a saloon, things like that. There are things I haven't seen; some instinctual events, pure from first flicker to final smoke, must, I thought as snakes slithered under the truck, still happen.

Outside Salt Lake the next day, however, more decisions were made for me. The most dangerous driver possible on these roadways, a woman in a bright yellow dress eating a chili dog with onions, and trying to execute, such a right word here, a left turn, turned into open-eyed me, head on. Glass broke.

At first I had been comforted by the fact that I had been standing still when assaulted and that there were a number of witnesses, but when I stepped out of the truck, the witnesses had transformed themselves into an unruly crowd. They were gathered around her since she was crying; everybody thought she was pretty badly hurt seeing all that chili on her yellow dress. When I heard them calling her by name, I realized I was in her neighborhood. I checked the damaged front end of my truck, and talked to her briefly while the mob stood behind her whispering dangerously. She was in incoherent grief for having ruined her dress. The whispering grew louder.

"Please," I said, "Won't you all cease casting these glances. This automotive tragedy is not my doing."

Hearing this the woman in the yellow dress wailed loudly and the crowd took a step forward.

"Okay, halt!" I said scurrying to the truck. "Forget it!" I called to the woman over the heads of the advancing villagers. In my rearview mirror I could see a dozen people noting my license number.

16

Easy access is a source for a major portion of all the grief and regret that blindingly swarm this planet. Even now on the remote edges of all the counted continents and the galaxies of islands surrounding them, human beings, not unlike you or I, sit facing the ice, mud, brick, or leaf walls of their homes, pressing remorseful fists into their eyesockets wondering why they ever allowed themselves close to places full of villains, like the Flying W. I took my truck to the grimy independent station called the Flying W Garage because of its convenient location, right next to the road, five miles from the woman in the yellow dress.

A fat man in a silver knit shirt bounded my way. He bore significant though uneven muttonchop sideburns. "An estimate," he said. "What is needed here is an estimate."

"Right you are, my fat brother." So from moment one, Nicky and I were at odds. He recoiled at my words Oliver Hardy style, then recovered and advanced in the massive swagger I was to see a thousand times in the next month.

"Now wait a minute, you brainless punk!"

"I need an estimate. Who do I see?" I wanted to take him, if I could, aback, talk business and forget my frank slip of tongue. He screwed his big face up in a convincing clench that then resolved softly into Nicky the Estimator.

"Well then, I'm Nicky of the Flying W Garage; I estimate things."

"Glad to make your acquaintance, brother." He circled the truck once and settled in front of the damage.

"Nice truck. Too bad."

"Chili dog."

"Three hundred and eighty dollars."

"Oh, you say."

"Plus any electrical work on this light."

I went around him and climbed in, closing the door gently but decisively. Click. "No way, Nicky." The Flying W didn't look that busy. I started the motor.

"Well there, partner, we could make a deal and fix up your nice truck."

"Wonderful. That's exactly what I need: a deal. But," I patted his fleshy hand which rested on the window frame, "I need a real, genuine deal, old Nick." He walked around the truck again looking in the rear and came back to the window.

"People who work here get discounts of up to fifty percent."

"They all must be just happy as little dogs."

"Two hundred dollars, and you can work here to pay it off. That is a deal, you know."

"You must be looking for a good man like me."

"The words from my mouth. What do you say?"

I got back out of the truck. "I say 'good' Nicky, when do I start?"

"Tomorrow. Eight in the morning. You can run the pumps. Plan on leaving the truck then too."

"Fine, partner."

It really wasn't any more strange than some of the job interviews I'd had before. When I applied to Blue Star Stamp Redemption Center they wanted to know if I was hypnotized easily. Seems a gang of clerks had hired a hypnotist and they had all the employees walking out in trances with radios and watches. Daily occurrences always strike me dead. But it suited me fine that I was going to be a gas pumper, a little of the old, you know, work. I did not care that my stab at this version of normality might be a little overt.

I arrived back at the apartment after parking my truck two blocks away and walking the rest. It was not your happy stroll; I had new resolves which like New Year's resolutions are not much comfort and the source of great doubt. I walked by Grinmaster's Taj Mahal Food Center, and his monstrous sign still rotated. At that time it was proof to me that life goes on. I'd been to Mexico and the grass had not been terrifically greener, but I would still stick to my new plans.

Eldon Robinson-Duff was taken unawares. "What? Here he is in the flesh, not one missive coming before, not a postcard from Nogales, not a telegram from Tucson?"

"Hello. I gave up. Mexico has been annexed."

"Gave up?"

"Couldn't settle. Too many things to do. Thousands of parties and no work. Also I ran out of fishing lures."

"Slow down. What happened?"

"Dotty."

"Oh no. No kidding?"

"In all actuality. So I've given all that up. Writing. I've begun a new life running into crazy women in Falcons and pumping gas out at the Flying W. I'm going to be normal, perhaps a cowboy."

"Really now?"

"Yes. Go ahead tell me. I've made worse decisions."

"Only one: Lenore."

"You got any beer in this joint?" I said heading for the kitchen.

"Wouldn't it be in the fridge?"

"Want one?"

"No."

I opened the can of Rocky Mountain and sat down looking at the idiot on the label. "How is Lenore?"

"Lenore is fine. She is engaged to the lice killer. She stops by from time to time to see me. She wants to know whether or not she should bring children into a world like this."

"What do you say?"

"She has no choice; this is the only world she's got. It looks like an October wedding. He's graduating, you know, unlike many other clear thinkers, and will be attending the counter with his father at an establishment known as Fair Deal Pharmacy."

"Good. He's a solid citizen and will . . ."

"Good! And you'll have your dream, the Ideal Lenore, right? You are crazy."

"Right, uh-huh. How's the book?"

"You're letting an amazing thing slip right through your fingers." He stopped a little pacing he'd gotten into and went to the desk. "The book's done."

"Going to publish?"

"No way. But you can look at it if you want." He threw me two full ream boxes. "It's the most extended truth I've ever told, and now thank god, it's gone."

"Too bad I don't have any war experiences, I might have been a writer too."

"You can have mine anytime." he said, scratching his helmet in a habit that had always distracted me. "That's like saying it's good we had slavery because we got jazz out of it eventually."

"Jazz is pretty good."

We talked for a long time, and though he felt I had made the right decision about school ("Relate it to anything, anything at all."), he wasn't sure about my future course. However, despite all news and advice, twisted and friendly, objective and acerbic, I could not move back in. Eldon was busy writing a piece on simple exercises to do while golfing for *The Sunset Gazette,* a weekly publication of Sunset Hills, a retirement community in New Mexico, and my continual awe of his red-helmeted figure sitting at the typewriter brought too much of my old life back home. And he, himself was not aiding my quest for new identity.

"Regardless of accents and that shirt," he grabbed the collar of a new red and brown cowboy shirt I was wearing, and pulled, snapping it open down the front, "you are not a gas-pumper and you are not a cowboy." People have a tendency to tell me what I am not.

"You don't know."

He grabbed my throat in both hands. "I know about you, yes I do. You need a new plan. One that makes sense, is inexpensive, and will offer you a sense of accomplishment in this world. Not in some twangy underground. Not in drugstores or rodeos. And not at the Flying W. It's nothing but a runthrough fence for every car stolen this side of Denver anyway."

"Leave me alone, Robinson-Duff. You're the one needs help."

"You," he pointed, still hopped up, "need guidance from above."

My philosophy is to believe things said in violence, especially phrases from old songs, but when he let go of my throat, I was still not convinced.

"Possibly later," was all I said.

17

For the extremely believable price of thirty-five dollars, I rented the ranch from Eddie, the ex–lion tamer who owned the Black Heron. After my revealing encounter with Eldon I stayed down at the Black Heron one night until closing and Eddie, hearing of my plight, fixed me up. It wasn't your standard ranch. The ranch house was a wheel-less airstream trailer that sat adjacent to the river on one side and the Union Pacific tracks that lead without hesitation to Wendover, Nevada, on the other. The trailer had been rolled, evidently, and consumed by fire, and (it was my conviction despite the relatively complete renovating job) hit by a speeding train. The very isolation of the ranch suited me, as did the spaces in the trailer. My bedroom ceiling rippled with irregularities and curved down toward my head like the sky. The kitchen-living-dining room had the kind of compactness that makes turning around mean entering a new room. Efficiency. The yard surrounding the trailer was knee high in June grass and assorted carnivorous wildflowers and full of horny toads. An old Studebaker was imbedded in the bank, nose in the river, as a monument to some narrow escape. All the doors stood permanently open, the occupants fled, and the whole brown thing looked like a huge flat dragonfly come to drink his fill.

Before moving in, I packed every artifact of my former life into cardboard boxes and took the whole load out to the dump. As I kicked them off into a sunset of smoke, bulldozers, and seagulls, I sang the chorus of a song called "A New Life" which I had composed in the clarity of the ride out. When my saddle oxfords flew out and down through the sun, as the D-12 cat lumbered by the truck, I felt the earth move.

For a while then, we have bucolic bliss. Eldon came by for dinner from time to time usually muttering, "Ranch, blanche!" But one day he came out with a trunk full of tomato plants, and as I helped him plant them near the Studebaker, which we sat inside sometimes, watching the river and talking, he said, "You've got to have crops in your stupid, confused Tex Ritter metaphor." I think he was sick of me referring to the toads as the livestock.

In the evenings as I sat on the metal trailer steps and watched the charcoal turn gray in an old kitchen sink I used for a hibachi, and the 7:50 grated by, spelling Santa Fe, Reno, Northern, Union, and all those other magnificent names, it occurred to me in my solitude that parts of my new life were far better than the strange brand of fretting and stewing that I had previously been engaged in. If the university wouldn't process me, fine.

18

I did feel bad about Lenore, not because of my investment, the hundreds of antic hours preparing and carrying off barrages of literary and artistic vaudeville, that is, in a way, fun, *but* because of my deep feeling, the nearest thing to a conviction I had, that you should marry the first person with whom you survive real danger. True, time and again I had created potentially disabling situations, crises, out of the most everyday of fabrics. I had forced her atop a Red Chief cab for a brief champagne spilling trip down a main street disappointingly lacking neon. I had pushed her, and she, me, into the city's fourteen fountains, including a small elaborate and uncomfortable one near the This is The Place Monument, in a three day campaign which led to exhilarating cleanliness and Lenore's serious cold. (Subsequently I had received an air mail letter from her parents in Minneapolis.) I had brought us to the brink, heightened picnics into survival training drills, made every stop at the Dairy Queen a turning point for all concerned, refused to settle for anything like your average retail experience, tried to make motoring into the adventure it should be. I had done these things consistently. I admit it. But it was courtship wasn't it? I had not been able to get us trapped in one of those rooms where suddenly the walls begin closing in vicelike, and one is saved in the ten inches by turning the oriental gong sideways, because, you'll be saddened to hear, there are no longer any such rooms. You can't even order one. It had been courtship, and I had tried in my simple ways to cement my relationship with the perfect Lenore solid. But I had failed.

"Why are we doing this?" she would say.

"Don't you expect us to?" I'd say, averting a forty-ton log with my paddle.

"No." became her answer more and more. I had failed, and nights as I lay in the bunkhouse underneath a rippled tin-can sky looking across at the diamond not as big as a Ritz cracker, I felt bad about losing Lenore.

But deep inside, deeper than could be spaded by my change of lives, my new immobile home ranch-type environment, my shucking of the adrenal past, I believed she had at moments enjoyed it. I believed I had given her things she would never get again, times, brilliant times that she would, even in a maternal and pharmaceutical future, remember. Perhaps I liked her being engaged to Gary, the graduate, the success, because she would remember going around with me, the bear killer, the saddleshoed, beachcomber midnight lost-and-by-the-wind-grieved poet-motorist, a dream obsessed monster, given to extremes that Gary could not touch with all the pills and potions in the state lined end to end . . . if I was not Gregory Peck in *Beloved Infidel,* then surely I was twenty million miles from home, wondering what next. In some ways, I thought then, in a late-night pathetic confidence, I have not failed, or given up on perfection.

19

After settling at the ranch, I called Proctor out at the power plant and he arranged for me to be the graveyard fill-in man, when someone needed to skip their shift. "How was Mexico?" he asked.

And I went to work at the Flying W. Nicky gave me two sets of light green work clothes that I really liked, despite the fact that the oval patch above the heart pocket was blank on one, and said "Ernie" on the other. On the back of the shirts in something like the Coors beer script, dark green letters read: The Flying W Garage. At this point in the link of events that I knew as my current life, things became extremely causal. I would have been better to have held on to my hat, so to speak. Like I said, I no longer blame big Nicky solely, but I should have been suspicious when they quickly pulled my only green truck into the garage right away and began the malicious tinkerings.

I was assigned to the pumps which I enjoyed a great deal. When the bells clanged their deafening clangs (it was really a clang!-cla-!, the second clang not quite making it) I knew with a reassuring certainty that they meant me. I learned quickly where the gas tank is on every make of car, front, back, hidden on the expensive cars, blatant on the trucks, hard to reach, convenient, and I took what was becoming pride in this simple knowledge. I bantered with motorists. Oil. Windshields. Water. Mileage. I was fast and friendly. But sitting in the office reading Nicky's greasy copies of *Bachelor* and *Layton's Auto Parts Catalogue,* listening to KTNT play truck-driver ballads, I should have been suspicious of Big Nicky and the Waynes as they whispered over my truck out in the garage. Then Paul Harvey came on and reported the news that Pierce and Van Buren the "Nevada Kidnappers" had been caught in Jackpot, and it was a great relief to me because hearing their names on the radio simply served my imagination up with great portions of those desperate Mexican evenings with Dotty. Good riddance to dangerous criminals.

I sat on Nicky's desk and watched them whisper around my truck. The three of them looked like three carnival ride operators whispering about the black gearbox of the tilt-a-whirl after a seventeen-year-old girl in a dress climbs aboard. From time to time they'd glance my way and I'd look back down at "Aurora," *Bachelor*'s glandularly disturbed foldout, while the radio played, "Kiss Me at the Wheel," a morbid song whose point was lost in shattering crescendos of twang. I should have been suspicious. But retrospect, like all weapons a sore loser, brandishes way too late, after the fight is over and all the combatants have gone home tired or injured to eat and rest and the battlefield is strewn with the bodies and innards of the sore loser's friends, sucks.

I didn't really like the Waynes from the beginning. They

treated me as if pumping gas were very like having scales for skin. They were Nicky's mechanics. Oh, they came in mornings and would say, "How's the kid today?" But I got the feeling it was because Nicky had told them to. Besides I overheard Wayne Hardell telling Nicky not to tell me about the bowling team. The other Wayne, Wayne Gunn, asked me dozens of times what my name was again, and when I told him, he'd say, "Okay, Ernie." and laugh a slim laugh. Actually he was a cheerless soul who, if you asked him if he had a match, would respond, "Who wants to know?"

I couldn't figure out what Darrel Teeth did or if he worked for Nicky at all. He came around quite often, driving a different car every time. One morning he pulled up and asked to see Nicky.

"He's right inside."

Since there was no business at the moment, I went back in with Teeth, whom I remembered seeing at the Black Heron where he hung out with Dr. Philosophy, Riddel. Nicky was inside stirring a load of powdered milk into his coffee as always with his screwdriver while he looked over the credit card slips as if they were marked cards.

"I need two more inspection stickers, Nicky," Teeth said.

"*Two* more?" Nicky counted to himself: "Two, Three, Five last week. It's getting tight when you want twenty a month, Darrel." Nicky looked at me. "Just a minute," he said to Darrel. "Larry, go out and give Wayne a hand."

I went out and stood by Wayne Hardell who stooped under a Saab, the only other car I'd seen them working on.

"Nicky told me to give you a hand," I said when Hardell looked up at my alien presence.

"Give me a hand!" He did a pretty good version of disgusted incredulity, "Why you wouldn't know pliers from a crescent."

He laughed at his own cleverness. "Go sweep the driveway. That thing over there is a broom."

"Listen you illiterate greaseball, I'm only interested in doing good honest work and learning what I can. I do not desire to be treated to these simpleminded insults."

Wayne hit me with the wrench.

I awoke from a dream of gasoline fires with a headache like a vice-grips on my head, and a full cauliflower ear. "Don't worry," Nicky was saying to me, "we've got workmen's compensation." I was experiencing difficulty in seeing straight. As far as I could tell I was lying in a pool of oil. I saw Nicky make a face to an apparition above me and Wayne Hardell loomed down.

"Sorry, big boy." He looked back at Nicky; then to me, "I lost my head." My head, full as an egg, was trying to hatch. "No hard feelings?"

I said nothing. Then Wayne was gone.

"Don't blame him." Nicky was talking fast. "His temper is crazy. Why he was in prison. You must consider this an unfortunate accident, like I said, the workmen's compensation. You're not mad are you, Larry boy? Your truck will be as good as new soon. We want you to like working here . . . why, you're doing a fine job."

Oh Nicky, you big fat bad man, if that were the worst, a short sleep and an ear full of blood, I could forgive and forget instantaneously, however that concussive event was only midstream in our struggles.

20

There were no more homicidal interludes at the station. Hardell avoided me and I him, and the other Wayne cast hateful glances around the place like jagged pieces of metal. He had the most expressive eyebrows I've ever seen.

One day Virgil Benson came in. He didn't need gas, but I topped off his tank (Volkswagen—in the hood) for forty-one cents. "Eldon told me I could find you out here, I wondered if maybe you want to see a couple of old movies out at the, Rainbow."

"Gee, I don't know, Virgil. I've kind of given up my analytical ways."

"That's what Eldon said. But these are great films."

"What are they?"

They turned out to be *Rhapsody in Blue* with Robert Alda as George Gershwin and *20,000 Years in Sing-Sing* with James Cagney and Bette Davis. They *were* great. I'll always remember if I ever make a movie to have the credits run across someone's hands on the keyboard, close up, and blast people out of their seats with beautiful music. In the other film Cagney took the rap for Davis and there was a beautiful, soft black and white scene near the end in which she actually visits his cell. At the very end, as they turn the electricity on, the prisoners file into superimposed view. The number of years each is in for flies off the screen and then the total appears in a crash of dramatic music: 20,000 years! Virgil and I went for beers afterward and it was pleasant for me to be in such clearly good company, but I made a vague resolve anyway, to avoid any other dangling ends of my former life.

Then one day DeLathaway came in. He needed a tire changed, and as I did the work we chewed over the demise of the couplet. He watched me the whole time, looking a little scared at what I had become. What he looked was "appalled." I understood all his weird behavior, but when he paid me and said, "There you go," it affected me. It is a fearful thing when people cease relating to you as your potential, and start talking to your actuality; it was too clear DeLathaway had lost any ideas of me being a perfect poet.

Being the rancher that I was I lost touch with Eldon and everybody else for a while, and then I began finding Eldon's articles in some magazines. There was a review of a Walt Disney movie, and a warm evaluation of Disney in general appeared in *The Utahn*. A lyrical piece on the value of winter appeared in the spring issue of *Mountain Calendar*. I was glad to see him succeed, though finding his writing in the various magazines was mildly distracting, like getting unsuspected mail, or phone calls at 4:00 A.M. when you try to make your voice clear and claim absurdly to have never been asleep. "Oh no, I was up . . . working." Things that send you into emotional U-turns.

Losing one's life can mean many things. At this stage in the outwardly placid Flying W game, I lost track, control, and significant other portions of my own. I've never seen a service station, garage, where more whispering went on than at Nicky's. I came to think the W stood for whispers. Nicky and Teeth had a little confab every two or three days; the Waynes were always at each other's ear out in the garage; and nearly every week a patrol car or two would pull in and Nicky would go out and lean on the window of the car and buzz with the cop for half an hour. I became pretty obviously in the way.

Nicky was getting as tired of asking me to "check the yard" as I was of strolling around outside with nothing to do. So I called him aside.

"Say Nicky?"

"Yeah, Larry boy?"

"Is there a lot of whispering during the swing shift? I mean do the employees gather in small groups of two and three and, you know, whisper?" Nicky himself thought it a good idea if I could change shifts.

"It's a promotion. You'll have your own keys and get to lock up."

"Oh boy, Nicky, gee whiz."

"Really, because I trust you so much."

"Wonderful."

"I mean it, Larry, honest."

So I started working alone, four to midnight, locking the joint up. Twice Proctor called and I went out to the power plant and disrupted the log until dawn. But mainly, I'd get off at twelve, go buy the papers and head for the Black Heron and drink beer until two when they closed. Darrel Teeth was there a lot with Riddel, but they ignored me. I think Riddel would have liked to talk with me a couple of times, but Teeth would steer him away. By two I would have formulated some kind of plan. I'd put more money in the juke box, D-7, Barbar Durrant singing "Leave of Absence," then exit while the music was still playing and hitchhike up to Lenore's apartment house where I would deposit cards, poems, letters, heads of lettuce, books, once a first edition of *This Side of Paradise,* and occasionally champagne in her car.

Once I procured four jars of poster paint and climbed up her trellis. I already had a vast landscape in mind, and it was looking very promising despite the fact that I had to paint everything backwards on the window, when a lights-out police car pulled up to the curb as Lenore and Alice, an older woman who lived in the building also, came out of the door. Lenore evidently had been able to hear the brush strokes on the window.

"You!" Alice said. She had learned over the past year a reasonable fear of what I might do next. The cop, Officer Sawyer, swaggered up the yard.

"Down here, buddy. Let's go." he said. I contemplated a paint spill, but then climbed down. "Oh," he echoed Alice, "It's you. Into prowling now, eh?"

"Look Mr. Sawyer," I said producing the paint and brushes, "I'm no prowler. These girls will vouch for me. Why she's my fiancee. We're in love." I looked at Lenore. She was luminous, standing there arms folded in her robe.

"Is that right?" the officer asked her.

"I know him. He's not a prowler, sir, sorry."

"No problem, ma'am." Sawyer turned to me. "But you, you watch your step. After all, it is two-thirty in the morning." When he had gone, I turned to the girls. "Sorry, I didn't mean to wake you." Alice started to go back in. "I really am sorry, Alice." She closed the door.

"She's still upset about the tupperware party."

"I thought they all got kind of a kick out of that."

"You would."

"Ah, Lenore, don't. I'm simply trying . . ."

"Larry, I'm engaged to Gary. I want you to stop leaving all that stuff in my car, and leave me alone."

"These are sentiments you don't mean. Didn't you get all the cards I sent you before I left for Mexico?" My tennis shoes were soaked from describing arcs in the wet lawn.

"Yes."

"Well?"

"I couldn't make sense of them." Her face was stern but showed that I had gained some ground.

"Well, you see, they . . ." She turned and gathering her robe with one hand ran into the house. The finality of such an act was viewed differently by the people involved.

21

I pumped gas at the Flying W for two weeks, when one late April night full of lilacs and gasoline, Nicky asked me the question that resulted in my literal incarceration, my one-year sentence. He came in one night about seven. Lila was driving. He was wearing his maroon doubleknits, broad white belt, white alligator shoes.

"Say, Boss Nicky, you're looking sharp."

"Nice, eh?"

"Yes, sir, need gas?"

"Hi Ernie!" Lila cried out across the seat to me.

"Naw," he said getting out. "Say, Larry, boy, can I borrow your truck? We're nearly finished with it."

"Sure, Nicky." I said looking down at the driver's legs. "Fine." That was my mistake. Maybe in a way what happened is my fault. Maybe. But blame is not the thing. It is not the thingee either, as Lila would say.

Lila was Nicky's sinuous girlfriend. Moll is a better word, and she came in the station all the time. I could tell her because she'd back and forth clang-clanga all over the bell cord, and I came to look forward to Lila's distracting visits.

One of the best aspects of working at the W, in general, was that I cleared my head. I began, as the university topsoil eroded from my mind, to think about one immediate thing: females. They drove by continually. Behind smokey windshields they adjusted the radio, lighted cigarettes, checked their hair in the mirror. Should I tell you I fantasized? Sitting in the office, up on the desk so I could see out, listening to KTNT broadcast the wrestling matches live from the fairgrounds, I composed an intricate series of dialogues. On bicycles, girls rode by wearing cut-off levis and red halter tops.

People it seemed, women specifically, were coming unsheathed. Older women, an odd concept, drove by in Fairlanes (gas tank, left rear) scratching themselves. Girls, unimaginably young cruised about, all windows down, jaws bucking on several generous portions of Doublemint. Kissing breath. The top forty a philosophy of life. They whizzed by bareback on the rear of motorcycles hugging their shirtless boyfriends, a siamese attraction. One day a lone girl in a loose yellow halter came into the station for air in her bike tires. I did not know how old she was, just that she probably didn't look that way last year. She taught me in a brief inflating minute that those handkerchief blouses were restructuring a girl-watcher's entire checklist. As she rode away, those long legs furious to be gone, breaking one of the state's longest ogles, I experienced a deep and pleasurable confusion. I developed the kind of imagination that could leap from an image of a young nubile pedestrian to the way her cut-off levis would look on the back of a chair. Mine, then, were simple concerns.

Also, in this connection, Wayne Gunn had a Marvin Auto Part calendar on the garage wall. It was one of those calendars showing a kind of hard-looking gal kneeling in an orange bathing suit. Of course, the bathing suit was only printed on the covering piece of transparent plastic, so when in a moment of chronological bewilderment, a person lifted the calendar's plastic (whoosh!), up went the orange suit, both parts, leaving the girl-woman who looked like a roller derby veteran anyway, in what can rightly be described as the raw. During slow periods you can already tell by my description of her, I'd stroll out in the empty garage and check the date. The calendar was for 1958.

So, I was clearing my mind. Monomania, really, is a simple disorder; the mind is pared and edited until only one superimportant thing remains. However, I was not obsessed, simply a very avid student of distaff humanity.

This is part of the reason Lila was such a thing. She'd ring all the bells and I'd run out. She would be sitting there, her short skirt barely reaching over. Sometimes not quite. Not quite. Then, while the gas was pumping, I'd do the windows and Lila would slump, sliding down and out of her skirt just enough, kind of bobbing to Sylvester True or somebody singing on KTNT. And there'd be triangles. That's what I'd see through the windshield: triangles down there. I always did a good job on the windshield.

So, a little dizzy from polishing glass and smelling gasoline, I looked up on the night in question, and there was dressed-up Nicky, nearly pinning me up against the turquoise T-Bird (gas tank under the rear license). He looked past me down through the reflections. "Can I borrow the truck, Larry boy? Couple of us are going fishing and I'd hate to take the Volks."

"Sure, Nicky." I said. "Fine." And I spun out of the vice against the car, still a little disoriented by Lila bopping now to Barbar Durrant's full blast version of "I Said Yes, Yes, Yes to Yesterday" which because of prior affinities was my favorite tune. I came to admire Durrant beyond reason which was where most of the other elements of my life resided.

"Where y'all going so duded up, Nick?" I said trying to reestablish a keel.

"To a lecture." he pronounced.

"On philosophy!" Lila yelled out the window.

"A lecture on *Work* by Professor H. A. Riddel, Ph.D. Ever heard of him?" Nicky reentered the automobile.

"No."

"Well, he's big, and we got special invites."

22

Lila always bothered me. One time she came in, you've already guessed this part, and bopped, riding her thighs down beneath her mini, until the triangle began to emerge, but instead of the little white soft high school pennant I was used to seeing, there was a good chance this time that she was . . . well. I can't be sure. Because at that moment, the gas overfilled, as it always did, and I rushed back. She was still laughing slightly when I returned, leaning left, right, left, in tune with Wayward Jonas Kline's "Truck and Trailer Mama." Oh Lila, sweet geometric baby of mine. Nicky's really. I began to form my own triangular philosophy of life on earth. She kept saying, "Ernie! Ernie!" Then when I'd come around, she'd point up to a spot on the window which I could never see, and say, "Get that nasty bug, oh get him now Ernie!" Then she'd point somewhere else, all the time bouncing in the seat like a woman on a spotted circus horse, everything around smelling warm and fragrant, hay and popcorn near the ring. But here, there was Lila, the rainbows of oil underfoot, triangles, invisible bugs, and the universal, sweet-acrid smell of gasoline.

And round Nicky borrowed my newly renovated truck and went south, fishing, with Darrel Teeth and the Waynes, which at the time I considered absolutely glowing, since Lila had been coming in a lot after four when she knew darn well Nicky was home.

And she never needed that much gas. Seems she'd put up her hair in these big rollers, and then go out for a drive to dry her hair and end up at the Flying W. So I'd rub her car, rocking it gently, and she'd slide down. Of course I got into the habit of teasing her, which is forward, I know, but when a guy gets himself an honest job, a new life, and a ranch by the river, he should be a little forward and make some opportunities happen for himself. It's like Barbar Durrant sings in "Classified Advertisement: Help Wanted Female," about how if there's a chance you better not fake it, grab it at the moment, get up and take it, and if there's not a chance make one before time (he says "tam") comes undone. I thought this was keen advice, especially in light of Wesson, Roachfield, and Royal and general skeptics revisited and what they'd put into my failing head. It also was close, in idea only, to what F. S. Fitzgerald had said at times. So I'd tease Lila when she'd pull up. She'd roll down her window and I'd say "white" or "blue," some color, and she'd smile out of her small face and say, "Ernie! Ernie! There's a big black bug on my window, Ernie!" I'd lean over and pretend to wipe the window, and she'd unsheath some pink ones. Looked like a little fire down there. I was going to offer to call the fire department, but my forwardness was still in the building stages.

"Nicky's going this weekend," she said one day. "Is he taking your truck?"

"Yes, they need it to go fishing. There's not enough room for Nicky alone in his Volks." Nicky bore an amusing resemblance to his own automobile.

"Well, you'll need a ride Friday night, won't you Ernie?"

"Sure, I suppose so." I had been hitchhiking without too many problems. "Aren't you going with our friend and counselor, Nicky?"

"No."

So, I was a little anticipatory, as they say, about the weekend's triangular possibilities, and let my truck drive away willingly. Perhaps, then, that moment of affected volition means the resultant mess was my fault. I don't know.

23

At twelve, Friday night, I closed the station and scrubbed up in the washroom, feet included, and put on my clean light greens. I selected the blank oval shirt, deciding perhaps tonight I would tell Lila my real name. The shirt was pressed hard the way uniforms are, almost like paper, but it smelled good, like baked soap, and my arms with their mild tan looked fine in it.

Lila came by and honked, because the bell was turned off and I locked the door and left. "Hi, Lila."

She didn't even ask me where I lived; she just swerved out into the midnight traffic and started passing cars headed out of town. Dale Henny was crying out, "Have You Lied?" at a sincere volume, so I waited until he finished, to ask skirt-straining Lila if she wanted to know where I lived.

"Oh! Can't we go to the movies, Ernie? I wanted to see the

movies." She turned left in front of a frowning set of headlights, and tires graveling, slipped under a marquee that spelled
out in multi-colored letters: TEN HORRORIFIC, FIEND-
ISH FILMS—ALL NIGHT SCARE SHOW. Smaller underneath that, it said: DOCTOR ON DUTY.

Lila paid the man and we coasted in, lights out, mound over
mound, creeping up to the second row where we parked alone.
The movie was in progress, that is, a man ran across the screen
with both hands up where his head should have been, and then,
headless, fell down. A woman came out of the shack behind
him with a bloody axe and one hand behind her back. We all
knew it was the guy's head. Everybody knew. "It's the guy's
head," I pointed out to Lila. Then the camera stared a slow
zoom in on the woman, while some violinists tortured their
fiddles to a heightened screech. They were getting ready to
show the head. The camera was still moving in slowly as if we
were all in it. The woman held the head up.

We all screamed. From some of us there were multiple
screams. Then the movie settled back into mindless boredom.

You must know that during our entire relationship, Lila's
and mine, which can be called in the pure sense of the word,
a charade, Scott Fitzgerald's advice on keeping one's distance
was filtering in phrases down on me. He had said to watch out
and not get too close to the carnival, regardless of how pretty
it appears from the distance. If you get too close you will feel
the heat and the sweat and lose the glitter of your illusions.
Perhaps, however, I told myself there, sitting inside that spot-
less windshield on the seat next to Lila, that's what I am in it
for this time. I had no trouble thinking of Scott's advice as
solely literary; that is, pretty, but not applicable in this case.

The second feature was a short documentary on the recent
evidence of werewolves in a suburb of Detroit. It consisted

mainly of women like the one on Wayne Gunn's see-through calendar lifting their skirts and revealing a variety of red and purple bites, while a breathy interviewer (off camera) asked them leading questions. The film had a certain way of supporting my budding monomania.

So just as they finished the credits which came down like a venetian blind across a still of a bitten thigh, I decided to make many of my most desperate imaginary service station dialogues into fact . . .

"Okay, Lila, let's get down to it, shall we?" It was a line out of one of Barbar Durrant's songs.

"Down to what?"

"It, baby, do not plead incredulity."

"Huh?"

"Come on, Lila, you know: white, blue, pink. And less than that."

"Ernie," she said warily, shifting farther away by the driver's door. "You behave yourself."

"Oh, yes ma'am," I said in pursuit. We were both behind the steering wheel now. "Like me to wipe your windows, ma'am?"

"Ernie!" I deftly probed pennant city. Her legs were very cool. "Ernie!" She slapped my cauliflower car. Soundly. Seventy thousand popcorn kernels marched down the screen, left-right-left, singing: "We are fresh! We are hot! Come and get us! Don't stop!", in cadence count, as blood swam hissingly over to the left side of my whirling head. Fifty hotdogs followed the popcorn, dancing a waggling chorus line to "Eat us! Eat us!" Above their heads, a Powerhouse candy bar flew over trailing a banner that read "Tasty Treats!", as the rainbow regiment of Dot-brand gum drops parachuted down: red, blue, green, black, yellow. For a horrific, fiendish moment, I thought

I might be in a car with Wayne Hardell. I looked over at Lila. She was mesmerized by the jamboree of colors and sweet treats on the screen.

"Ernie? Ernie?" she said sounding quite sincere, almost using her old get-that-bug voice. "Ernie, can I have some popcorn? I want some popcorn." I was trying to inhale and align my eyes.

They zoomed in to the green nodes of a talking pickle next. He was dressed as a professor in a cap and gown, and he was reasoning with us to really take a chance, buy a pickle and have an astounding taste delight.

"Ernie?"

"Lawrence. My name is not Ernie, it's Lawrence, and I want you to call me Lawrence from this moment unto eternity, which I suspect may arrive presently. Lawrence. Lawrence. Got it, babe?"

"Yes," she said with satisfying meekness.

"Okay, I'll proceed to get the popcorn. Perhaps it will elevate you onto the sexual plateau that matches my expectations, or if not perhaps you will throttle on one of the cute little kernels."

"Huh?" she said. It is times like that that assure me I have unadmirable qualities. While I was attempting to stand erect outside her Thunderbird and a pizza loomed large on the screen like a pocked moon, pepperoni and green peppers to go, Lila leaned over conciliatorily and patted my hand. "Gee I didn't mean to hurt you, but I didn't think you'd be a Dr. Jekyll and Mr. Hyde. Nicky's my main man."

"Right." I started to walk back to the snack bar.

Came the voice: "Butter!"

"What?"

"Get buttered popcorn, Ernie!"

Naturally, it was at the snack bar where I felt the heat and smelled the sweat, and really, much more than that, amid the malevolent faces of the general public. Several women bore the pale, tired expressions and wrinkled blouses of the recently assaulted, and they filed resignedly in and out of the Ladies. I selected a fistfight with a huge man who thought I had crowded in line, which I had, but I growled and sighed my way out of it as if it were my third or fourth for the evening. And I bought popcorn and, logically, a pickle.

The checkout girl, a fifteen-year-old blonde in a dirty white dress, sat on a small stool so that her legs led into a not so mysterious triangular shadow. I asked her where the doctor was.

"Doctor?"

"Yes. The Doctor on Duty."

"Oh. Well, you better see the manager. Back around this building, in the booth."

"Fine. Thanks."

The manager was also the projectionist. He was hoisting reels onto a table and sweating to extremes. "Shit!" he said after the last load of reels was stacked up. Above his head, the monstrous projector ground out a massive, intense beam, and the film clacked.

"You're going to be up late," I said.

"You're goddamned right I am."

"Listen, I need to see the Doctor on Duty."

"Who?"

"The Doctor on Duty. Don't tell me you're also the Doctor on Duty." He finally looked at me.

"Why do you need to see the Doctor on Duty?"

"Well," I started using my breath more and speaking up and down, "that horrid second feature. You know, the one about Detroit."

"Yeah."

"Well, I used to live there, and that third girl's story scared me so much . . . well, I passed out and fell out of my car."

"Listen, Mac, are you putting me on?" He took a step toward me.

"Look." I thrust my ear up at his sweating face.

"Holy hell!"

"And if I can just see the Doctor on Duty I'd feel a lot better . . ." I was near tears.

"Sure, Mac, sure. Well he's not here right now. Called away. But what we do is give you your money back, and you can call your own doctor from your own phone, eh?"

"WHAT DO YOU MEAN THE DOCTOR ON DUTY IS NOT ON DUTY!" I screamed. "I'll sue this run-down gravel quarry! Waahhh!" I started wailing. Just then the reel ended and started whipping itself to shreds in the big machine, and the car horns started erupting throughout the drive-in.

"Holy hell!" he cried running back to the projector, cutting his hand on the berserk spinning wheel. Outside it sounded like 5:00 P.M. in New York City. He got the next reel running on projector two, but couldn't stop big number one, and finally while it spit splinters of film up and down the room like sharp rain, he turned back to me. He glared and slapped a ten in my hand.

"What!" I said over all growling machines, "Ten bucks? For my head!"

"Quiet will ya, Mac?" He handed me ten more and I left him as that hot room filled with filmic confetti. From all I can ascertain, people in this world relate that way: striking from the lashes of bad faith and threatening each other with legal action.

On the way back to the car I stumbled into Dotty's Mercedes. Back in town already. I could tell it was hers by the mashed back fender. Someone sat up in the back seat, but I hurried away. I could see the fourth feature was nearly over. It consisted predominantly of people breathing quite heavily, leaning on doors they'd just slammed.

"Where have you been with my popcorn?"

"Pipe down. No interrogatives, please. Slide over, we're going home."

"Nooooo. No! I want to see the show!"

"You've seen it, sister."

"You just be nice to me, or I'll tell Nicky." It was an effective thing to say.

"Fine, I'll be nice, but we're going home."

"Oh look, Ernie, the previews!"

It was true, the multi-colored spotlights and swirling letters congealed to spell out COMING ATTRACTIONS, and though my whole thinking was desperate to flee, there is something about previews that will always hold me, perhaps a drowning hope that the future actually does hold something in store. I don't know. So I sat still for a minute, eating professor pickle.

The previews were for next week's SKIN-FEST—A PORNUCOPIA OF FLESHLY DELIGHTS." The future. A naked man chased two naked women through a meadow while a bass-voiced announcer suggested, "Love can be *natural.*" An interior shot disclosed four naked people on a bed aggravating each other. Then, in an office cut, two secretaries ripped each other's clothes off, tearing away blouses like newspaper, strangling each other with their bras. Then two bank robbers made everyone in a bank strip, and while they looted the cash drawers, the customers started in on each other. The fundamental theme of the pornucopia seemed to be that if you could get the secretary, bank teller, or schoolteacher to remove her glasses, she suddenly would become a voluptuous nymphomaniac, shaking her hair down from its prudent bun into a sensuous mane, and generally bumping and grinding all over the place. This bit of optometric psychology interested me only so far: Lila didn't wear glasses in the first place. Maybe I could have gone and borrowed a pair.

After that steamy bit of the shape of things to come, I once again renewed my interest in my old friend, Lila, but only half-heartedly. Seeing Dotty's car had sat on me heavily; you know, mistakes you've made and would like to erase, and besides Lila smelled strongly like a regiment of popcorn by now. The previews had been right in one respect: they accurately predicted a sad, sordid, confusing future that was at that moment, as Nicky and the hoods clambered over my truck in the troubled abdomen of southern Utah, laying undisputed claim to me.

So I gave up on Lila; it wasn't a very noble dream to begin with. As *Son of Dr. Jekyll* started, I turned on the highbeams and roared out, taking the speaker and cord with me, cutting off the manager-projectionist's voice, "The snack bar will close in . . ."

I had Lila drop me off three blocks from the ranch, because I didn't want anyone but Eldon to know where I lived.

"Why here, Ernie?"

"I'm going, my dear, to throw myself in yonder river. Goodbye." As she drove off, a relief swept me that made the idea of seeing her again, of searching for her first among all the world's citizenry, of risking my fissile neck in order to talk to her once more, absurd. I obviously did not know that she would be the key to the impending quagmire, or that I'd be in jail by dawn.

24

There was a note on the bunkhouse door:

Power Plant. Larry, where are you? E.

I checked my watch: 8:00 A.M. Holy smoke. Hitching out to
the plant was slow business, but I got there an hour later, at
five, met the boiler roar, and found Eldon tapping ashes into
Popular Mechanics.

"Do you know that a guy from St. George named Figg has
patented a one-man boat made out of discarded car hoods?"

"Gee, really?" What was he talking about?

"Listen!" He showed me the page with the photo and dia-
gram. "But according to a fellow name of Thomas Deerfly, a
Uinta chief who runs the package store in Duchesne, and who
I interviewed yesterday, he invented the damn thing."

"Amazing, this copyright interest in Indians you have."

"I've been interviewing them for two weeks on a thing for
the *Bridgerland News,* and there's a lot of shit going on like
this. I'd like to meet this Figg guy."

"You becoming an investigative reporter? Humphrey Bogart
in . . ."

"*Deadline U.S.A.* Maybe. I don't know." He looked up and
closed his magazine, pressing ashes for eternity. "Where have
you been? When Proctor called I went over and waited at the
ranch."

"Seeing a doctor about my ear."

"Fine, but send me a check when you get paid, all right?"

After he left I circled the boilers for an hour awash in the deafening blast, feeling bad about the typical angle my new life had taken. I did not want things to get complicated. Face it, I did not want them to get in the least bit hard. I think I was ready for a few hobgoblins to enter my little mind. Then I went downstairs but all the ginger ale was gone. A few coins rattled in the white plastic drawer. Upstairs I vitriolically noted in the log that this consistent and demoralizing pilfering of other's ginger ale was surely going to lead to the break up of society as we know it. I didn't note that that would probably be a good thing. Then I turned to the back of the huge log and tore out the page labeled October 12, Columbus Day. On it I scrawled in my most florid hand:

> Dearest Lenore,
>
> On this day, staffed with seventy diseased dangerous convicts and general do-badders, I touched upon the fresh green breast of what is called the New World. It was a rough trip, what with all the spoiled apples et cetera, but now I have done it, and I dedicate my discovery of the world being round to you. I knew it all along. Soon all kinds of people will be able to travel this short cut to Dubuque and Albuquerque, just to name two full of u's. Also Utah. You know, I wasn't really looking for India after all, just you. The continent is populated now with cut-throats and escapees, won't you marry me? You are the gem of the oceans. Cordially.
>
> Larry Columbus.

After sealing that for mailing, I checked the big board. This is when the single orange light of my blighted fate blinked amid a sea of blue. I double-checked. Reset and checked again. The light was Beaver, Utah, and I called Proctor at home at six-thirty in the morning, not knowing that the orange light meant that Big Nicky and the Waynes and Darrel Teeth had not gone fishing at all. Instead they had gone to steal copper wire in southern Utah with my truck. They had cut down one *live* wire with three miles of valuable copper wire they were clipping from an abandoned line in that county, and in this nocturnal process they had shot a watchman right through his pickup truck. In effect then, I was turning myself in, and would be in the hands of the proper authorities in less than two hours. I should have known Nicky wasn't going fishing; he couldn't stand handling worms.

25

Nicky had left the Waynes and Teeth off in Gunnison where they had the Saab waiting. Nicky had continued north in my truck full of copper wire. When the highway patrol pulled him over in American Fork and charged him with grand larceny and attempted homicide, he quietly listed me as his accomplice. The man he shot, Hatcher Kinnel, was in the hospital in fair condition with a bullet hole entirely through his shoulder. "Why, they tried to assassinate me!", the papers reported him repeatedly saying.

Nicky, being used to this lifestyle of shabby illegality, acquired Darrel Teeth's lawyer, bail, and a suspended sentence in that order and in a hurry. They'd been through this six times before for various felonious endeavors and they knew the cops, the judge, the ropes.

Then it was me.

26

It wasn't at all like the movies, and I, myself, it turns out, was nothing like James Cagney, except I did learn, waiting through all the black boredom of my trial, to smoke cigarettes like food, like a deep blood need. It seemed that Lila was in Elko, Nevada, indefinitely and Nicky's "Sure it's his truck," didn't aid matters. After I'd told what there was of my tale to what there was of a judge, my incredulity slowly congealed into an unmagnificent indifference. I mean how could I understand dozens of human beings pointing things at me as I came and went from the courthouse? Fists, fingers, cameras, microphones, and I suspect somewhere, a sharp pointed stick or two.

Mrs. Kinnel, the injured man's wife was there evidently; I think she was the spleening woman who screamed, "Assassin! Assassin!" as I entered the room. Mrs. Ellis for some acrimonious reason was there also. She didn't yell anything; her presence was barb enough. She had, her face announced, been expecting something like this of me for a long, long time. Riddel was not there. Eldon because of his helmet was barred from the gallery. I sent him a note, finally, that said: "Please water the tomatoes. Cordially, Larry and Vanzetti." I won't go on. That all things are possible became gradually apparent to me as all the papers were shuffled and filed so thoroughly against me, and I, myself, amid a pointed crowd, and cries of "Assassin! Assassin!" was conveyed off to the Big House.

I loved calling it that during the trial: the Big House. In the courtroom I'd turn to Nicky, who was perversely benevolent enough to attend, and say secretly, absurdly, "Hey, big boy,

don't you worry, things'll be different up at the Big House."
Yes, that was before. Let me tell you something: no one in the
Big House calls it that anymore.

Giving Vaughn, the bald checking guard my clothes and
raging watch in exchange for the "garb" as my new wardrobe
was called, I said, "So . . . this is the Big House, eh?"

"What?"

"So, this is the Big House." I repeated looking around at the
corners of the pale green room as if I were looking clear across
Montana.

"Oh," he said. "You dumb-ass. You sad dumb-ass." He
shook his head. "This is goddamn prison, and you're in it." I
stopped saying that for a while. The rest was like that too: My
dreams of prison fell away, heck, they were ripped away like a
shirt in that porn film called *The Secretaries*. There is, in the
end nothing romantic about having no toilet seat.

At dinner we filed in cafeteria style and were dished ade-
quate, lukewarm food by Doug, Fred, and Star. The head cook
was my old acquaintance Leeland Rose, DeLathaway's help.
We sat in small groups and talked, and again I am not telling
lies, about the weather. The cups were styrofoam and no one
ever pounded his on the tables which were small, pastel ovals.
The whole scene was so stinking, so disappointing. It reeked
of the casual.

Back during the theatre of the absurd, the trial, I had
thought occasionally, fine if this vicissitude among others is
visited on me, fine, another new life of extremes. Wrong was
I. We'd actually loiter after the ham casserole lunches, smoking and breaking our styrofoam cups apart slowly, gently, the
way a schoolteacher would, and then at the sound of the
moderated whistle which did not blare, but sounded, (like
Muzak stuck on a xylophone note), we'd break up and go to

work. I certainly would have rather had Mrs. Hatcher Kinnel, wife of the "assassinated" man, sneak up on me while I lounged in my swimming pool and drill me full of complete holes from an oversize pistol. Some kind of dramatic ending would have suited me much better, a conclusive and final event, despite the fact that I would have had to borrow someone else's swimming pool. At Mrs. Ellis's, we didn't have one.

Frankly, I also expected everyone to be filing and refiling his case with teams of hip, longhaired lawyers who came and went on motorcycles, because naturally, every prisoner had been wrongly accused, tried, and convicted. I couldn't wait to get next to any of this injustice, so I could get myself the same lawyers, and commence the real wheels of justice. After all, right is right.

No one said anything about lawyers, cases, anything.

I stood in a long line of men the fourth day waiting to see Mr. Smelter, the Vocational Rehabilitation Officer. No one talked about their lawyers. We stood in a comfortable, accepted silence. I kind of liked the shuffling, when the line moved up one man, shuffle, shuffle, but unfortunately there was no grumbling to accompany it. That we were all guilty or innocent, the same as all the pedestrians strolling freely about the metropolitan walkways, tilling the rural soil, or leaving motel rooms in the baked sunslant of afternoon, was simply a becalmed piece of data, a cold fact. The boredom drove everybody places they might not have gone otherwise, but we were all—innocent (myself, remember?) and guilty—in the same backseat.

I tried to assume the stance of the men around me: one leg at a time shifting, cigarettes dropping from mouths like smouldering caterpillars quietly to the cement floor. And soon I too, was standing as though this was any line, registration, car wash, hamburger, matinee, urinal at the ball park; soon I too was doing the great American one-step, the act in which all people in free countries spend most of their time: loitering.

It got so I kept wanting to clean my wallet, which was locked away somewhere in that complex in a manila envelope, to sort the old restaurant cards from the newspaper clippings, from the phone numbers. I thought back to that woman in Why, Arizona—lady, you were right. There is no better reason. What we were doing in that line, like everybody-everywhere, was serving time. Now there's a concept.

Then Mr. Smelter's mahogany door opened and it was my turn. His office was full of metallic knick-knacks, that upon closer examination showed themselves to be parts of broken tools: shards of broken shovels, rake teeth, screwdriver handles. A polished crowbar, bent into an N, weighed down the papers in his "Out" basket. The bookends were the heads of two hoes. Mr. Smelter looked at a stiff white card that must have been about me.

"Wire, eh?"

"Sir?"

"Interested in electronics?" He leaned up on his desk and picked up a smashed hammer head, feeling its weight.

"Lightning only." He put down the hammer head definitely and leaned back and blew up at a mobile of burnished broken saw blades. It began to turn slowly.

Still looking at it, he asked me: "Well, Boosinger, tell me. Do you prefer to take two things and make them into one thing, or do you prefer to take one thing and make it into two things?"

"I prefer . . ."

"What?" He blew upward again. There are some questions in this world for which I do not have the answers, and so I looked blankly at Mr. Smelter who really was unfit to give advice to the lovelorn, which I guess I was, really. "Well, what do you say?"

"That's a great question you've asked," was all I said.

"Okay, then," he said after a silent saw-twisting minute, "landscape maintenance." I stood up. "Report to Spike in the East Yard right after lunch." I left him there as he probed his ear with the single leg of a shattered pliers.

27

I started going to work in the East Yard. My budding best friend and next-door neighbor, Salvatore, worked in the laundry and he said I had a pretty good deal working out in the sun. I had been assigned to the landscape crew for the new wing which was being constructed as we shoveled. We were scribing out a contoured bed for small fitzers which would serve as an organic transition between the walls and the yard.

The East Yard was mostly centerfield for Dexter Diamond, the prison's hardball field, where we played Sunday, Tuesday, and Thursday afternoons. The foreman of our crew was a triple murderer named Spike Spike, a red-headed former strong man at the circus. I've never seen a grown man with so many freckles. He kind of liked me and gave me the pleasant chore of turning the sod in the bed mixing in the topsoil with a pretty good Acme Land Company shovel. My soft foot got pretty tough right under the arch where I'd jump on the shovel, driving it into that rare prison soil.

So May passed, and I was assumed by prison life, which as

I have said, was just a life. Work in the yard, smoking in the cell, talking evenings with Salvatore, playing the fiercest kind of baseball, no real hassles. Can you believe it has come to this in this country's prisons?

One thing I should confess that I had expected to happen was my auction: you know, the new greenhorn (they don't use that term either), the young guy comes into prison, and all the hardened criminals cluster like a boil around him bidding with smuggled dope for the fresh flesh. My first weeks in the block, even at work, everybody ignored me. I tell you it was just like the world. And no one asked me what I was in for, ever. I had "Oh, you know, assassination," all ready for them, but no one was interested.

Spike turned out to be a good man, very helpful in the field and proud of the work our crew was doing. He came over to me one day and said quietly, "You know, Larry, my name isn't really *Spike* Spike."

"No?"

"No. It's *Randy* Spike."

"Randy, huh?"

"Yeah, but I don't like anyone to call me that." He set his mouth. "It's a kid's name." He looked at me through nine million freckles. It was the most amazing confession I've ever heard. "But you can call me Randy if you want—just don't let anyone hear you, okay?"

"Okay, Randy."

"After all," he said kicking a clod into dust, "It is my name."

What I liked the most was the baseball. Getting off early those three days a week, playing the games, was incredibly pleasant. The teams had been cleverly named, proving the presence of intelligent people on that particular side of bars. My team was the "Dangerous Convicts." Good, right? There were seven other teams in the league, but the only one that was a real threat to our squad's taking the title was the "Escapees," which as you can see is a clever name also.

As a team we Dangerous Convicts had spirit, but the games were quiet. We'd all sit on the bench like tired people at a dentist's office, not talking much, but on the field everybody ran the bases and fielded the ball at dangerous velocities. No one made jokes about stealing bases, even to Lefty, who had successfully robbed eighty-one banks, all in California. Off the diamond we rarely talked to each other (except for Salvatore who played second and me, the third baseman); and even the most omniscient of observers would have had trouble telling we were a winning and somehow unified team.

Aside from that and the extensive vocational guidance and rehabilitory aid the prison offered in the person of Mr. Smelter, there were also two courses being given that summer for high school or university credit. "Body Movement: Grace" was the title of one, "Poetry Workshop" the other. I decided to take "Body Movement: Grace" because it had to be good for me and anyway teaching body movement in a prison is the kind of paradox that attracts me. Unfortunately, the instructor Roland Pound emphasized the Grace more than the Body Movement. His thesis was that a fundamental requirement of grace is never to look at your hands. Never. He showed us how to walk and sit down, and in a way it did good things to our convicted postures. But I only stayed in the course two days. It wasn't because of the cuts I got shaving while I stared directly into my own worried eyes. It wasn't due to those moments in class when I'd sit down on a hand and not be sure if it was my own. I quit because of the third time I lit the filter on one of my cigarettes and took a death-defying drag on all that nylon-fiberglass et cetera. In that third hacking moment as cough moved to retch, I decided to once again start peeking at what my hands were doing. Besides, the whole concept played hell with my infielding.

To compensate for dropping grace, I enrolled late in the poetry workshop which Salvatore had already told me Wesson himself was teaching. I considered wearing a disguise for a while, but then dropped it and just went in to take my medicine. Wesson was as incredible, or is it credible, as everyone else. He delivered his knowing glance in my direction for a moment and then started the class, not knowing he'd soon be drawn across the keen edge of our imprisoned imaginations. He read a poem by some character I'd never heard of, some "friend" of his, during which Wilkes, a grand larcenist from Grand Rapids, kept saying "Hey, teach, if this is a workshop, where are the tools?" The first two times he said it everybody laughed, but Wesson continued reading using his inspired baritone voice. The only part of the poem we could hear was about this guy leaving Reno for San Diego and the promise of the West, a new life, or some such geographical lie.

"Hey! Hold on!" Lefty yelled out.

"Good. Do you have a comment, Mr. Croisure?"

"Yeah, I got a comment." He addressed the class: "Look, the guy says he's leaving Reno, right?"

"Right." Wesson put in. "For the site of new promise . . ."

"No way! I worked in Reno for six months once as a backup dealer. God, there was this girl worked in front of me. Some piece! Rode her bike to work . . ."

"Yes, yes, and . . ." The class ignored Wesson's prompting.

Lefty went on: "Wendy was her name. Rode her bike . . ." Here Lefty lapsed into a blank-eyed reverie, and the class, we sat in respectful quiet in our circle. "Yeah," Lefty came to, "this cross-eyed poet needs a roadmap. You don't wait to get to Reno to go to San Diego. Why you can't get there from Reno. He'd have turned left in Elko!" The class exploded in hoorays and applause.

"Lefty should know," our coach, Oliver Panghurst, added, "he's been there."

"And so I conclude," Lefty concluded, "that this here poem is full of shit." More wild applause.

"Ahem, yes, well . . . the idea of promise, of moving west," Wesson was faltering, "of starting a new life, certainly is not lost on you, you . . ." Oh Wesson, you are hanging over the abyss, ". . . you confined-type men." Wesson collapsed on the lectern.

"Us confined-type men," Lefty spoke for everyone, "find this kind, like any kind of shit, offensive. It's the goddamned poet who's lost. He *ought* to start a new life as a . . ."

"As a prison guard!" Panghurst shouted.

"Yes!" Lefty came back. "*Yes*, as a prison guard—that don't take no brains!" The room, like so many I'd been in of late, disintegrated into descending debris, rising smoke and splinters of light as paper clips streamed silver toward Wesson's shock-white eyeballs.

So I stopped going to the workshop, though Salvatore reported to me from time to time and it was clear that Wesson was being dealt the kind of cards he deserved. I know this moralistic stance here seems inappropriate, but Wesson had openly rubbed me what is known as the wrong way too long, and revenge, regardless what nonsense is uttered by rehabilitation officials and other coxcombs, is nectar, and who—given the choice—won't sample a smidgen?

28

At night still, I'd lie in my bed, but I couldn't believe I'd made it. In the period before sleep when people do their best thinking and from which no thought is recoverable, my mind slipped through the successive holes of thought faster and faster, like a car's motor racing after it has stopped, the whirling centrifugal whine, metal against metal, all oil gone up in spires of tinged steam, and the clutch, wouldn't you know it, in. That is to say, among the other fifty billion thoughts that flew by like bats in the cave of my indignant rage, I thought about my own responsibility and guilt. I had felt guilty before about different things, so I knew what it should feel like if it came. I had had black-hearted moods, entire atmospheres of guilt, in which conscience like a drunken lumberman fed the long planks of my raw remorse to the sawblade; but I didn't feel that way now. At all. Perhaps it was the deep sense of embarrassment I felt for all the hundreds of paper readers and civil employees who thought I was guilty that led me onto that trackless train of thought, onto that rapid-fire midnight docket. The sentences flew out like the years in *20,000 Years in Sing Sing:*

> For ever knowing and associating with Dorothy "Dotty" Everest—five years and a thousand-dollar fine, fine suspended because of Mexican penalties paid . . .
>
> For various croquet felonies—two years . . .
>
> For not marrying the perfect Lenore and buying a small orchard farm in Logan, Utah, and, don't you know, settling down—five

big years . . . with this sentence came the conflicting maxims,
"It's never too late" and "Don't close the barn door after the
horse has fled." It might not be too late . . .

For not punching Mrs. Ellis's son-in-law—six months . . .

For ever gaining (what a word) employment at the Flying W
and existing within the same square mile as the Waynes and
Teeth—five years at least . . .

For coveting the vanished Lila—a clear five years . . .

For not taking more drastic measures with Lila—six months
. . .

I ransacked the rest of the potentially guilty clutter in the
desk drawer of my mind, but really couldn't come up with any
regrettable details that I hadn't already paid for, except an
incident at the Pumpkin Hop which took place with my close
associate at the time, Joylene North. That was way back in
junior high, and I assigned myself ninety days for it.

As my thought processes closed down for the night and sleep
approached like the wolves around a diminishing campfire, I
added all the debts. Twenty-four years and ninety days. Sub-
tracting my age, I had only sixty-six days left to serve. I was
determined to serve only sixty-six days more. I rolled onto my
back and looked up at Bette Davis who knelt concernedly over
my imprisoned self, and I said, "Sixty-six more days in Sing-
Sing, baby, and I'll be coming home." I fell deeply asleep
twenty minutes before the dark night of the soul.

29

Summer passed. I worked hard on the fitzer beds, and took firm pride along with Randy Spike in the job we were doing. Days are such small items. They merged and streamed by. It was like those scenes in the movies where they show the superimposed calendar being torn away, page by page, and blowing off into the wind. June. July. August. They also have the newspaper come spinning out at you and then it slows and stops and one headline says JOE ELECTED MAYOR; then another paper spins out at you, stops and says JOE ELECTED GOVERNOR; then a third comes spiraling out: JOE ELECTED PRESIDENT. And you know that suddenly Joe has made the big time, as they begin a shot in the oval office, and that he has forgotten all his old, dear friends. It doesn't take long, movies tell us, for good people, the kind you and I know, to become crooks. Well, in the prison it was the same. Time whirled away and by late August the "Dangerous Convicts" were tied for the league lead with the "Escapees." We'd have had the title clinched except our best hurler, Armstrong, got paroled; the best hitter in the league, our centerfielder Manny Bloomfield had been some-what eviscerated in a knife fight; and our first baseman Enos Harper had escaped by walking away from the farm detail.

Despite these handicaps our coach, the red-faced Oliver Panghurst, along with the rest of us, still felt confident that we could win the league. The announcement was made that Sniffy Laughton was making a solid brass trophy three-feet tall and weighing nearly ninety pounds for the winning squad. Sniffy ran the machine shop. That was when our team started eating lunch together, quietly talking, breaking our cups apart slowly like bread; that was when things started getting more realistic, or unrealistic, as the case may be, and things had a chance of making the movies, of going beyond this confined mediocrity, well, that is to say, we planned the escape.

It was mildly unfortunate that we didn't use phrases like, "Yeah, we're really going to blow this joint!", when talking about the escape, and the general conversational tone was disappointing also. No one growled in a hysterical rasp. Perhaps it was because the plan was simple. Simple and easy. Just having the escape was enough for me. I didn't really care how they talked about it. Deeds, that ran around breaking down doors, were in order, not Words that twisted into nothingness like smoke.

The plan. The new wing would not be completed until early October, and until that time all of our air vents were open ended in the new unfinished system. From there through one set of corridor bars, through the basement passageway, out the side doors, across the budding fitzer bed, onto centerfield of Dexter, and over the wall. I got all the information about the new wing out of Spike as we'd talk during the day.

It became obvious from the first that he would never go for escaping until the landscaping was done. I felt bad about prying stuff out: "Where does that door go, Randy?" But it was escape wasn't it? And he liked leaning on his shovel and talking about the way things were going to be, the master plans for the yard, and his role in it. Besides, our route took us right through the fresh fitzer beds, as I've said, and that would have killed old Spike. So I didn't tell him anything.

"Going over that wall is going to be one hairy mother." Wilkes, the pitcher, would say three times every lunch. "You got the beam. You got the guardhouse. The guards have got machine guns." The guardhouse beam we measured, and it swung around the yard, just like in the movies, every nineteen seconds. "It's gonna take two-three minutes to get the eleven of us over that mother wall. It's gonna be hairy."

"Okay, you Dangerous Convicts," Coach Panghurst said over his plastic tray, "Somebody has got to go down there tonight and clear that set of bars out, and check those East Yard doors." He smiled, tapping his spoon on his cube of green jello. "I've escaped four times and been shot five, and if we get hung up between here and centerfield, we are gonna get our Dangerous Convict asses shot off, and I'd personally rather be in prison than," he stopped tapping and stabbed the spoon into the green quivering mass, "be dead."

There was a thoughtful jello silence.

"I'll do it."

I said that.

That afternoon I received a letter from Eldon. He had been looking for Lila in my behalf, but she hadn't turned up.

Dear Larry,

They closed the Flying W, and Nicky and the gang have moved over to Roosevelt for other felonies. Don't worry, I am on the case. . . . I've kept what stakeout I could at Lila's place for the last week: nothing. If she shows, I'll get the necessary evidence, confession, or flesh. Will a pound do? Lenore came over about three weeks ago, and your dreams will be happy to hear she cried. Heavily. But Gary is very in the picture: marriage.

I am now contributing editor to *The Guide to Fishing in Eastern Utah.* I've met some wonderful Indians while fishing, including an incredible guide: name of Nighthorse. Many fish leap from little streams calling your name. Don't worry, I don't write about the good places. The tomatoes are thick, but green. How about coming to help with the harvest? Many more events to report, including Indian lore, but later . . . . . .

Your pal, Eldon

P.S. I have a new roommate and it is hilarious.

Despite the impending jailbreak, as I chose to refer to it, the news that Lila was not coming forth bothered me enough to make me misplay a bunt that afternoon. I started in way too late, and the Felons spoiled Wilkes's shutout. We still won seven to one. But all through the game I could not repress stomach-sinking thoughts about the bad faith Lila was wielding against me by doing the worst black deed: nothing. Where was she?

That night I sat smoking in my cell watching the grid of moonlight slide in a closing parallelogram over the floor. As it was about to slide a little bit onto the wall, I got up and into the garb still barefoot. I tenderly lifted the vent cover which I had loosened in the after dinner free period, and I stared into the opening which was about the size of a book. It was all getting worthwhile. I thought of Nicky missing out on all this due to his untimely acquittal. I climbed into the minute door and started getting stuck immediately. That shot me enough adrenalin to inch like the mad mole, onward, even around a corner, and seventy feet further where I came right out into this earth's sweet atmosphere and, incidentally, into the new wing.

The empty unfinished wing of a prison at night, stark and barren, is not unlike its finished counterpart, full of maligned American citizens such as my friends. I walked, strolled casually, swinging my arms, down the corridor to the last cell and the row of bars we had to get through. Now a wall of bars is more than a concept; it is a thing. Putting my hands on the long black bars in the dark, they seemed solid. Steel. I'd seen (you have too) those guys in movies stand bewildered behind bars and shake or, ha ha, try to shake the bars, crying in what is called anguish. I did that without the crying. The bars were firm. I did it a little more, making the facial expressions of an innocent man locked in the clink, which it occurred to me, without a tinge of irony, I was. I shook my head and stretched my face quite well into: frustration, sadness, anger. Then I did some combinations: Angry frustration; Helpless frustration; Raging insane anger. During that one as I bucked against the bars, I let out a little cry and suddenly stood pointedly still. "What was that noise?"

When I realized it was I, I went back to wild sadness, clinging to the bars making mouths as if I had my fingers in the corners. As I raged, near tears, sinking slowly to the floor, Bette Davis standing right on the other side, one of the long bars came loose and I was sitting on the floor holding it like the first man to invent the spear. All facial contortions stopped and I did a very convincing version of abject surprise.

The concrete was not firm; the bars had not set up yet.

I had stopped saying "unbelievable" at the trial, but I thought it again there in the dark, laying the bar down without a clink. I slipped through the space, and bounced merrily down the stairs to the East Yard doors. The latch hadn't been installed yet, but the two doors were chained together at their handles. I pushed them tenderly outward until the chain was taut. There was a space of about two inches, through which I could see part of the prison wall, beyond that, mountains, beyond them, stars. But only two inches. Not even enough for the human mole. Even Salvatore, that skinny greaser, couldn't slip through. As I stood there thinking, "Okay, Lila, maybe you'll change your tune when you see this Dangerous Convict face to face; there are things in need of rectifying," I saw another thing appear in that two-inch gap: a nose. As it poked in, there was an accompanying growl speckled violently with saliva from one great big dog, a german shepherd, looking in to see who's messing. Deftly I pulled the vision closed, carefully allowing "Wolf" to extract his nose. A big dog. I replaced the key bar in its sandy socket on my way out and returned, after another tangle with the tunnel, to my cell. There under the thinnest membrane of sleep I dreamed of walking through a desert of broken glass that glistened like teeth.

30

The next morning at work while Randy Spike was cleaning the teeth of the red harrow we used to level the grounds, I went back to the newly finished beds. Each little shrub was surrounded by a wet circle where it had been watered. Using my most canine of imaginations, I scratched a reasonable amount of damage into that ordered surface. I hated to do it.

Back at work on the unfinished portion of the beds with my Acme Land Company shovel in hand and constantly underfoot, I stopped Randy when he came by and said, "Darn it, Randy, that german shepherd they keep in the yard nights is a headache."

"What do you mean?"

"That damn dog is wrecking the bushes!"

"Where?" he said, dropping his shovel on the spot. I showed

him and he went away, nearly at a run, toward the office. After another short while, I saw him coming across the yard with Mel Trammel, our yard officer and prison guard. I continued turning the sod as they talked. When Randy returned I asked him what happened.

"They're keeping that god-damned dog in the kennel tonight. Trammel says the dog's been shitting out near shortstop too. Probably just a case of not being fully trained."

"I'll go straighten out the mess." I said.

"Thanks, Larry, that's great of you."

"No problem, Randy," I said, choking up on the shovel and carrying it like a bat over to the recent landscape violation. After work, I very carefully, in studied negligence, leaned my shovel against the East Yard doors and ran off, gleefully, to play ball. It was the afternoon of the sixty-sixth day.

There was a big crowd for the game, all the other teams came to see us duel the Escapees. Even some of the off-duty guards came out, standing just out of play like dark final umpires. Panghurst was really excited. His face was redder than usual and he went around to each of us saying, "Now or never, boys." We all knew it was our last game, not because the season was ending, but because, we hoped, tonight we were leaving the league. "Now or never, Larry."

"Right."

"You know," he said privately to me as we sat on the bench in the second inning, "I hate to leave. I'm not sure there's anybody here qualified to take over the license shop." He was foreman of the license plate shop.

"They'll find somebody."

"Naw," he said, taking off his cap and running his finger around the inside rim, "I'm not sure. It takes a mastery of phonetics. You wait, if we pull this thing off tonight, license

plates from here on will go straight to boredom. It takes phonetics." Panghurst did have a point. His masterpieces were a
rallying point for all citizens who'd ever been in the prison. The
state's plates were three letters then three numbers. He did a
famous series consisting of thousands of FCK, PHK, and FUQ.
He plated ten thousand OWP which were his initials, not to
mention his BFD's, ETC's. He was clearly the best plater in
the country. My truck plates, I recalled, had been OWP. "I'm
just not sure anyone else knows enough phonetics, Larry. I
mean as soon as they start making DIP or GOD they'll get
caught and some straight guy will be shipped in who will avoid
all meanings. Then what have you got. Yeah," he said, snug-
ging the cap back on grimly, "the job requires a thorough
understanding of phonetics, and a measure of subtlety."

Right then, a rapist from Pocatello who played for the Escapees hit a two-run homerun. It broke the guardhouse window
and so received more cheers than it should have. Panghurst got
up and went down the bench. "Come on you guys; it's now or
never."

Lefty got on in the fourth and stole around to third. Then
Wilkes popped to shallow right, but Lefty tagged up and made
it in anyway. That made it two to one. In the eighth, I got a
Texas league single, and made second on a passed ball. Two of
our ace hitters struck out. Then Salvatore hit a line drive
exactly down the leftfield line and I scored on his double. Tied
up. The dispute over the fair-ball call on the play led to an
extended fistfight between Lamar, our 300-pound new first-
base man and the Escapees' left-fielder and shortstop, the
Nevada kidnappers, Pierce and VanBuren. The rest of us stood
in our places while they rolled around and around. Every time
Lamar would roll over one of the guys, the entire crowd would
groan for him. The two Escapees kept trying to get up and

fistfight, but Lamar snared them into his specialty: wrestling. The fight finally was stopped by Spike, when the three combatants tumbled too near the shrubbery. He poked them with his shovel.

The game remained tied until the eleventh inning, when Lamar got trapped between first and second and the Escapees got so involved in the run down that Leeland Rose scored easily from second. There was wild cheering in the twilight, and I found it a little sad as we shuffled away from the empty Dexter. As the triangular period of my life came to an end, so too the diamond era passed.

During dinner a rat-a-tat-tat started up and everybody looked up from their trays for a minute fearing the everlasting machine-gun moment, until we realized it was raining. After dinner the Dangerous Convicts sat around two pink tables in sullen fashion, picking their cups apart depositing each piece in the middle like a coin.

"Rain."

"Yeah."

At 1:00 A.M. we met in the new wing, each team member emerging from the small mouth of the vent like a word in a secret. I removed the bar, not bothering to play Superman, thinking all the while, this is really it: escape. Wilkes kept whispering scared little things about being shot to death. He wouldn't just say, "shot," no, it had to be, "Shot to death."

"Wish that goddamned light would go out."

"That wall's going to be one hairy mother."

We filed through the opening in the bars in batting order, which is already how we'd agreed to go over the wall. But at the East Yard doors I led out and pushed the doors against the chain. Straight as a loose bar in a prison, for instance, the handle of my shovel fell through those two wide inches. A moment later, after applying one of the seven basic tools, shovel as lever, the doors were open and centerfield lay before us under falling rain. I could hear everybody take an involuntary breath when the doors swung open. On the wall two hundred feet away, the beam's dripping white circle passed back and forth. The Dangerous Convicts stood in the doorway posing as if for their group photo, breathing, looking out at what occurred to them to be the future. Exactly, precisely, at this moment, I thought, like the movies.

"Good luck, Salvatore," I whispered.

When the light passed again we ran across the muddy yard. Ah, Spike, I am sorry. The beam got there just before we did and passed cleanly away. The wall was wet. We boosted the first three guys over the wall handily, but Sammy Watt, the clean-up hitter, slipped, and four of us landed in a body pile in the mud. We all stood up again, just in time to get thoroughly clipped by the big beam. Sammy climbed upon Lamar's shoulders this time, slipped again and the light slapped us.

Wilkes said, "We're dead." What a cheerful body.

The light was coming back again, but we had Watt and the fifth hitter Leeland Rose on the wall; machine-gun fire was imminent. The light waved past twice more as we groaned Lamar up the wall. Each time it would come it was like death. It seemed to slow down when it would focus on us. I got on the wall and reached down for the last four Dangerous Convicts. Salvatore got over easily and then we hoisted Panghurst out of turn. He deserved it. He sat up on the wall by me for a moment inhaling heavily. "Good luck, kid," he said.

"Thanks, Coach." He dropped to the other side and I looked down at the last two Dangerous Convicts. One was a pinch hitter whose hitting ability depended solely on the availability of certain drugs which there had been a drought of recently, and the other was the batting practice pitcher. Getting the pitcher over was hardest. He kept slipping and hitting his chin against the wall. On our third attempt, as I hauled him up I could see his chin bleeding badly as he winced up into the rain. Then he slipped and fell hard against the wall and, snap! I heard his jaw break, and he went out and down like the ten-ton anchor weighing down our disaster. The beam flashed on us again as I looked down at our unconscious pitcher. The other Dangerous Convicts had scattered in the fields. And in a moment I gave up all hope of escaping and clearing my name, and dropped quietly down beside him in the rain. As the light came by forty more times while I brought him to, I learned to stop worrying about it, and I stopped flinching when it came. I stood up straight, and we took our time, helping each other over the wall. Sitting on top, straddling that long horse, I looked back at the beam mad as I could be. Can you believe things are like this in our prisons in the United States of America today?

No one was watching.

I dropped to the other side of prison walls and ran as one of the Dangerous Convicts away in rain falling like soft bullets.

31

There is no activity so stimulating as running away from prison. I leaped, stride by stride, up a grassy slope avoiding every quick snake through the trustee cherry orchard and across the four-lane highway. I stopped on the far side of the road.

It was comforting to be standing next to a road again. There was no traffic. The rain was half snow now and thickening in the dark. The first attempt at a storm of the fall. The trusties were weeping in their shanties over the damaged cherry crop. I raised and lowered my arms a few times: this is my body, redelivered. Then I threw myself dramatically down the gravel incline of the highway and sneaked, stepped into the first convenient post-prison culvert to think about the next thing.

It was about four-feet high and I ducked in and sat down the way you should in a sports car, knees up, and leaned my head back against the rough brushed cement. It was pleasant to be out of the recent precipitation, to be breathing in this round sanctuary. I hadn't run so far since high school when I intercepted one of Skyline's passes in the end zone and ran it back, slalomming the field back and forth with the help of that wily guard, Boyd Marsing, to the nineteen: an eighty-one yard run. I could see my breath, a broad plume, in the culvert and in the light at the far end of the tube I could see snow falling. After a moment I felt I was in a simple round elevator, rising through snow. The dizziness passed and I focused. Scratched in the curved wall opposite me were several sets of initials and dates —B. T., W. D., G. C.—and beside them this legend: "This is the first place they'll look! Get out and don't hitchhike!" Someone had also taken the time to draw a picture of a large submachine gun. Heh. Heh. I picked up a jagged rock from the culvert bottom and wondered what I should add. Looking again at the shifting snow outside the porthole I called, "Okay Fitzgerald, what should it be, given this once in a lifetime opportunity? Come-on, Scott, you devil, what's it going to be?" There was no real or imagined answer. Inevitably, what I was doing and where I was doing it were what Scott would have considered relatively low life. Few things glimmered. Finally I

133

scrawled "The Scottsboro Boys, all nine of us!" and underneath, "411", which was my batting average, and which you
know is not bad in any league.

I felt like scratching some angry news about how disappointing these prison escapes really are and how things are appar-
ently in general decline. Don't mistake me: I'd rather be alive
than shot or even partially shot, wouldn't you? But once in a
while someone should look up from the strangling void of their
own misery to see dangerous criminals climbing the wall. I
guess. I couldn't figure how to get that all into a rhyming
couplet, and so I let it go.

There was a noise outside the culvert, a noise like teeth on
a sandy clam, and a small animal ran across my lap and kept
right on to his next life out the other end. I hoped it was a
rabbit. The noise, a grinding, continued and as slowly as my
returning heartbeat came the beam of the flashing light.

I am apprehended, I thought. Someone has missed me and
I am apprehended. The proper authorities have checked my
vacant cell and found my bed badly stuffed with a workshirt
imitation of myself, and they have apprehended me. It was
convenient being in the culvert, then, because it gave me only
two options as to which way I should run. I chose to follow the
rabbit, and crawled the eighty feet to the other side and
stepped out into the flat world. The light, a yellow beacon,
flashed in flecks on the snow, approaching, and I appropriately,
I thought, raised my hands and mounted the roadway. The
blinking beacon pulsed nearer and nearer as the police car's
headlights lensed the falling snow. I could smell the snow in
my hair. Here I am standing in the oddest snowfall of the year,
reaching for the sky, which can never be a bad ambition.

I wondered if they had caught Panghurst, that wonderful
crook, or Salvatore. It would not be that clever to be the first

or only one caught. I hoped they had caught at least six others so we could raise a team again; you can play with seven but you must forfeit with six. What if I were the *only* one captured? I could see the felons moving away from me on the bleachers; oh and then it struck: Spike. Oh, devils in heaven, Spike would commit his fourth murder and this one with good reason. "Listen, Randy, I'm sorry about the fitzers . . ." No, I was had in that regard. Once a man has taken the risk of telling you his name, betrayal, say trampling his bushes and leaving him in landscape solitude, is unforgivable. He would rake me thoroughly into the dirt and trample me; it would be an environmental mayhem. He would tamp me fatally with a shovel. He would perforate me with a rake.

The flasher on the monstrous police car pulsed up to where I stood, arms aloft, in snow, and then ground right past. It became a snowplow. I blinked and lowered my arms and watched the huge truck move away, like a steamboat.

My incredulity took several seconds to settle as I stood calmly on the highway looking down at the lights of the prison. It looked like a minor constellation of stars. I could see the circling beacon wave my way once every little while, fooling no one, and suddenly I was running again. I remember the culvert's carved advice: don't hitchhike, but if I could catch that grinding snowplow . . .

After I fell the second time on the slick gathering and melting snow, I was back in my Boyd Marsing football runback reverie. Everytime I breathe hard, I think of intercepting that pass in front of Inez LaNonca and 700 pubescent fans. She could breathe also, if my memory, that bastard, fails me not. After two hundred yards I caught up with the slow-moving truck. As I approached the tailgate where I thought I'd hop on, a stiff ream of sand slapped me in the face, eyes, teeth. Argh.

I stumbled to my knees on the ice and spitting sand, felt the thick perfume of truck exhaust. In a second I was up again and learning by my mistakes for once, hooray, I ran up to and alongside of the truck. I grabbed one of the canvas stays on the side box of the truck, and pulled myself up beyond the five-foot tires waiting to tread on me. Stepping drunkenly, like a man fallen off a trapeze onto the safety net, I found a corner of the canvas covering the tons of sand the plow carried, and crawled underneath. The sand was dry and felt warm. With the grinding softened by the sand, and the safe smell of canvas, and the simple monotonous vibrations of the truck as it cleared the road back toward Salt Lake, I thought two inconsequential thoughts about Lila, and went into sleep on that strange humming shore.

I've never been one of those people who think it important to wake out of a dream and write it all down before it evaporates. The people who do this feel that otherwise they will miss out on a third of their lives. My own feeling is that we should pay attention to what goes on, but when we're out, leaning on one of the shelves of the comatose, high or low, we should *be out*. If a dream is important, it will come around for you later as you're putting the keys in the car or ordering coffee; you'll recall your mother with the hatchet over your cradle, or your family waving from their side as the earth splits massively in half. I also think it appropriate that one day when I'm sixty, I'll wake up and realize I've slept twenty years, which was enough for Rip Van Winkle, and looking around with everything changed under my feet in my own town (even perhaps my progeny, those surprised heirs, will be different), I'll have to nod then and say, "Yup, yup, guess I was asleep." It's the only way we can rectify the large changes that move our lives away from us. As a child I awoke to find the seasons changed.

Snow on the clothesline. So I don't think we sleep to rest, but to swallow. The raveled sleeve of everything is knit, and I'm not interested in chasing up those wispy alleys of semiconscious scheming known as dreams and writing them down. This is a long way to say that I should have dreamed under that canvas on that sand aboard that truck of sleeping on the last dune before a troubled ocean. Umbrellas. As is, as you can tell, I did not dream but passed out in a dark attempt to get over not being shot out of my pants escaping from prison.

WHEEEEEEERRNNNN!

The brakes closed, and I awakened. The truck dipped and jolted down three tortuous inclines and stopped. The motor quit, and I heard the door slam. And echo. It sounded as if we were in a cavern.

32

After the driver's footsteps faded, I looked out from under the canvas. It was some sort of underground garage, and there was a neat row of trucks parked in their snowplow line. I climbed out of the sand and rappelled down the side of the huge truck, standing finally on cement firma shaking sand out of my loose trouser legs, and listening. The machines all ticked and dripped as they warmed and cooled, settling. Once in awhile I could hear the wet crash of an iceberg as the snow clods under the wheel wells fell to the floor. First snow falls in this lifetime. Each crash sounded like a sneeze. After the initial fear passed, the fear that doesn't allow you to move, I moved to the front of the truck, then skipped back and up into the cab. The little fears ran up and down my legs now like adrenalin. Over both visors were pouches of pens and pencils. The driver was probably a writer. In the glove compartment there was a pair of gloves; a copy of *Calling All Cars*, a mystery by Duke Milk; and an old package of Pall Malls. I took the Pall Malls as a favor to their rightful owner, and then found the pair of overalls under the passenger-side seat. They were crumpled and white, but looked official. I couldn't find a hat.

I explored the basement, walking around in the wrinkled white suit trying to look rightfully tired after a hard night of plowing. The mouth of the cave was sealed with an electronic mesh gate. There was no switch on the inside, and I contemplated for a minute how much easier it would be to roll away a large rock. At the other end, one hundred yards away, was a caged section labeled: M.V.C. Through the chain-link fence in the darker portions of the garage, I could see rows and rows of tagged used cars.

Walking along the chain-link enclosure further, I saw my own used truck. I stopped, shocked by this new voltage, my mouth trembling involuntarily, and no words. "You too," I wanted to say, hating this surprise, "They've got you too!" I thought of my watch and wallet locked in lockers at the prison; the new penal theory being that if you lock up a guy's stuff, you've really got him. My truck waited like a good horse back three rows, and its windshield stared back at me. This is sadness, I thought then, firming my jaw, teeth locked, in the confirmation of my resolves to haul the negligent Lila forward onto the proper witness stand. I tried to hum then, to dissolve the lump assembling in my throat, because music is one of the verities ("There'll always be music!"), but after a few wavering bars I recognized the tune as one of Barbar Durrant's melodies: "Lost without a Compass in Your Love" and I let it die, settling instead for the choking throat clot.

Trying to turn self-pity into anger can at times resemble falling off a log; it is just not that hard. By the time a tear ticks the nose: done.

I found an elevator around a cement corner. I descended and opened, empty. I entered and looked back across the space at my truck. "Don't worry, big fella, I'll be back," I said as the door closed. As the elevator ascended, I felt again the ancient worry of being hoisted into the arms of the law. I smoothed the overalls and tried to look authentic. That failed so I tried to look tired. I mastered this fairly well, although I know part of my face still read: This man is scared out of whatever wits he once had and should be wrestled to the ground.

The door opened and across the vast marble hall I read: METROPOLITAN HALL OF JUSTICE. I couldn't move. The doors closed again. They opened and a policewoman carrying a bouquet of parking tickets walked briskly inside. The doors closed. I rode with her to the third floor where she marched off in her blue skirt, and a person in what are called plainclothes entered. We went back down to one, and when he waited for me to exit, I did. If he hadn't made the gesture, I might be there still. As I shuffled down the steps of the Hall of Justice, in my own custody, into a night lightened by a minor dusting of snow, it bothered me again that those people didn't know who I was. Perhaps they had the news already that I was innocent. Let it pass, Larry, I thought, shake it off. Let's get Lila.

33

After a brief tangle with a phone book, I walked the sixteen blocks to Lila's apartment. I thought it was only right not to call ahead. At this early hour, she'd be sure to be home.

Lila lived in Whilewillow Village, not a village at all but a large, multi-unit, cubist, prefab, apartment building surrounded by sixty hedges designed to hide all the seams. The architect involved in Whilewillow Village lives somewhere else, and comfortably on the money he should have been divorced from in a malpractice suit. After I located the front entrance, which was closer to the rear, I climbed to the fourth floor and knocked loudly on Lila's door. I was debating whether to open with: "Remember me?" or "Okay, you shit, we're going to tell the police about being at the drive-in; come on," when the door opened and Wayne Hardell pulled me into the apartment. Oh la.

Big Nicky, looking bigger than ever was seated on the brown sofa, and Wayne Gunn sat next to him looking at the pictures in *T.V. Star Magazine*. Hardell shut the door.

"Hey, Larry. How you doing? We heard your name on the radio tonight." Nicky said. He was wearing his triple knits again, a light green leisure suit. The shirt had vast triangular collars which framed his florid face like a platter.

"No doubt. You're looking relatively sporty, Nicky, I hope your presence here portends the assistance I seek." No one said anything. The tangible sense of assault and battery was in the air. It was one of those situations where to cope one needs to have been drinking. Since it was all thin ice anyway, I skated

on: "Look fellas, friends, and former colleagues, I need a grain
of assistance . . . by the way thanks for all the cards and letters,
flowers, and news, while I was in prison . . . Nicky, I thought
you of all people would try to send out a file . . . Listen, I simply
want to clear my name and to be reunited with my recently
abused truck once again. I've been fleeing things and serving
your time, going backwards long enough. If the credible trio
of yourselves, or Lila, or Darrel Teeth, would step up and tell
them where and why I was while you were climbing telephone
poles in Beaver and shooting at strangers, why then I could
begin again going nearly forward with this malady known hu-
morously as my life. Come on, Nicky, please."

They said nothing. I counted them: one, two, three. Wayne
Hardell stood out of the hunker he was keeping beside Nicky
and moved to the window indifferently, like a man looking for
a bus. Then he walked behind me to the door and squinted at
all of us. Since he was the only thing moving in the room we
all watched him. When he turned, I looked at Nicky.

"Oh shit, Nicky."

"Yeah, I hate this stuff," the fat man said. "I have to leave,
Larry." He was the one buffer between me and the unspoiled
meanness of the Waynes.

"Oh, shit."

Nick pushed and lifted himself out of the couch and
squirmed for awhile pulling the green knit slacks out of the
crevice of his awesome rear-end, saying, "Larry, oh Larry. We
want you to not ask us these things. We want you to forget.
We don't know what you are talking about." He opened his
arms in a gesture of sincerity and honesty, those things, and
then he smiled. "We thank you for your help and we hope you
have learned something while you were at the facilities."

"Prison, Nick, prison, from which I had to escape risking my neck in order to be treated to this? Look, Nick," it was time to plead, "My fiancee, a girl who received from me the same affection you bear the noble Lila, will never communicate with me again unless my name is made clean."

"Many men, Larry, are far happier as bachelors. Goodbye."

"Where's Lila, Nicky?"

"Who?"

"Oh, I see."

"Goodbye, Larry, I don't want to see you again." Nicky walked to the door; Hardell held it open for him.

"Nick, oh shit. Instruct your fine apprentice here not to strike me with any metal objects, wrenches, for instance."

"I'm just happy we were able to capture you before you committed further crimes against society. Bye, bye." Hardell closed the door on this portion of my possibilities and turned, facing me.

"Come on, Wayne, don't squint at me that way. We're colleagues, remember?" I moved back before he stepped on me. He wanted to hit me pretty badly. It had been hard on him waiting while Nick and I negotiated.

Wayne Gunn said: "Come on, we can't stay." He indicated me with his forefinger while looking at Hardell. "Do this." Hardell stepped for me again.

Hardell kicked me. I couldn't believe it. It was a sharp kick with the toe of his wing tip and I could feel the skin barked. "Oh, kick me, you big man," was all I could manage. My cleverness was up to its neck in fear. Hardell was five inches taller than I.

"Knock him out and let's go." Gunn said.

Hardell hit me in the face. I took it on the right cheek bone, and it knocked me down. I then made the mistake of springing right back up. I did it, I suppose, to assure myself that I was still alive. My temper, also, that odd monster of emotion I rarely glimpse, rose finally like the dripping head of Godzilla from Tokyo harbor, ready to bite.

"Look, you crooks," my voice broke to a tenor as I danced, hands out, beyond kicking range, "crimes have been committed; I did not commit . . ." There was a serious shortage in the room of heavy objects such as lead pipes or candlesticks for me to raise and strike villains with. "And you mindless bastards did. And we know it! Everyone in this room knows. Now . . ." Gunn stepped on the sofa cutting off my last escape. Absurdly, I raised the phone book at them. "Watch out!" I yelled. It was a pretty good yell. As the book fell open in my hand, no friend's number in sight, Hardell jump-stepped and socked my forehead. My head hit the wall instantly, and Gunn lowered an entire mahogany coffee table on the part in my raised hair. True, I had not yet begun to etcetera when the lights inked, and my body followed my wilting clothing to the floor. Through the murky canvas of unconsciousness, I thought I could hear Wayne Gunn phoning the police. I kept hearing the word, "whereabouts," "whereabouts," and then the busy signal and the distant ringing.

34

I awoke in Lila's apartment at dawn. My neck was sore when I moved it one way, and as I ran my hand over the muscles I felt the stiff brown line of caked blood that led up through my hair to a new tender extrusion on my scalp. It was as big as the Ritz. Every time I pressed it with my fingers, my eyes closed involuntarily. For a moment I felt like the last true phrenologist: "Son, your skull tells me that your life has become distorted." Then my leg began to sting where I had been kicked.

Ah violence, that cleanser. We do not solve our problems, we kill them. Wrenches and tables are more instrumental in problem-solving than psychiatrists will ever be. "Violence," from "vio" (Latin) meaning wooden club, bludgeon, and "lence" meaning the hands of a villain, my head, no help. I sat on the floor, opening and closing my eyes, waiting for things to become lovely again. Then I remembered the police.

Had Wayne Gunn called? Would they be here any minute? Are they here now? I jumped up to look out the window, and sat suddenly down again. Then the blood came back and I stood up. The bulge on my scalp felt as if it would burst. I still hadn't heard my name on the bullhorn: "Okay Larry, come out. Throw down the machine gun. We know you're in there!"

Outside the snow had melted except for the crescents on a few car tops. The police did not have the place surrounded. No one had the place surrounded. The streets were clear. A woman stood at leash-end nonchalantly looking the other way while her twin Saint Bernards had their massive holiday near the front tire of one of the parked cars. I could hear birds recovering from the snow, ready to continue now with the last of summer.

The police had not come, which did not surprise me. It does not seem to be a causal world.

I washed my face and noted Lila's cosmetics arranged like a minor city on the counter in the bathroom. She still lived here all right; just not when I was around. Nicky saw to that. Rubbing my face with the towel I started to feel better: brash and healthy like the escaped convict that I was. I could also sense renewal in that I was getting angry.

I dialed the police and stuck a corner of the towel in my mouth.

"Hello?"

"Hello," I said. "This is Larry Boosinger. Have there been any calls for me?"

"Hello, Hello?"

"Hello! This is Larry Boosinger. You know, I escaped from the pen last night, and I wondered why the police haven't answered the call they received . . ."

"Hello, sir, you'll have to speak more clearly."

I pulled the towel out of my mouth.

"Hello, sir, can you speak just a little slower."

I hung up. They are trying to ignore me, I thought. They are not even tracing the call. They probably do not trace calls anymore. I was supposed to be wanted by the police. I went back to the window and looked at the empty street where the woman was being dragged away by her two monumental house-pets. It was another brand-new day, and I wasn't going to blow it.

I called Eldon and let it ring thirty times. A voice answered: "Kenny here." The new roommate.

"Where's Eldon?"

"Right here. Hold on."

"Hello?" It was Eldon's voice.

"What do you think of the third as compared to the first person?"

"Christ, what happened?"

"I'm at large."

"You don't sound any different. Where are you?"

"Whilewillow Village. I'll be the citizen in overalls standing in front."

"Moustache?"

"Not yet. Hey. Bring some of my clothes."

I left a note taped to Lila's mirror:

Call the police and tell them that we were at *Werewolves in Detroit* the night Nicky stole the wire and that I knew nothing of Big Nick's plans for my truck or you will not ever go to Heaven that bower where we all receive our due rewards.
Menacingly, Larry Innocent Boosinger.

Twenty minutes later Eldon picked me up in his car.

"I shouldn't do this," he said. "Most hitchhikers are ex-convicts."

"Most folks are criminals too. How are you?"

"Fine. Let's go fishing." he said. His helmet seemed the perfect artifact of homecoming.

"Might as well. Prison escape, poaching. It's all the same."

"Escape, oh boy! Fill me in."

So I told him the sandy, lumpy, twisted historical romance of the last twenty-four hours. When I finished, he was silent. He looked at me, his mouth a line. I felt suddenly vulnerable, uncertain of what to add. It must have been how he felt returning from the hospital. I remembered how we'd joked about the skull brace he wore. I finally had talked him into throwing the gruesome thing away, and we went downtown in February to purchase a football helmet. I'd wanted one with wings or ram's horns on it, but, since it was the off season, we'd had to settle for the red one. In the street right after he'd put it on (I made him), he said, "Are you sure about this?"

"I am if it's you in there."

Now, in his car, I looked at his mouth which began to quaver. Then: the laughter. He laughed and laughed until I laughed briefly at his laughing. There were tears from laughing, and he had to pull over as he couldn't breathe from laughing.

"This is funny. This is very funny," I said. "You can stop laughing; there is no goddamned reward."

"A table. A coffee table." He arched back in the seat and laughed extremely, making only a little noise. Then he put his hand on my head and felt the bump. "Not bad. You should wear a helmet." Collapsing again.

"Are you going to be all right?" I said. "I mean do you want me to drive so you can enjoy yourself?"

"Hello, Larry," he answered. "It is so goddamned fine to see you again."

"On behalf of my head, I'd like to say that it is very fine to be here."

The sun was on the edge of the Wasatch Front, and the shadows were receding on the far side of the valley. The barren Oquirrh Mountains were becoming golden.

"You have arrived just in time for the fun," Eldon said.

"Meaning what?"

This." He reached into the backseat which as always was littered with novels, biographies, and newspapers, and he handed me a page of the newspaper. He pointed to a half-page ad.

I read: "GRAND SLAM STOCK CAR DEMOLITION DRAG RACE SPECTACULAR!! Uinta Raceway proudly announces the finale of the season. ALL or NOTHING for more than a dozen famous entrants. See Championship Crashdriving as that Daring Demo Duo Gunn and Hardell take on the Lone Racer Darrel Teeth in a Knock Down! Tow Away! Demo Derby! Bring the whole family to see these Daredevils. Slams! Bangs! Thrills!" The race was scheduled in two days.

"Gunn, Hardell, and Teeth!" I looked at Eldon.

"Yes, and I'll bet Nicky and Lila as well. I was afraid I'd be going to the races alone." He smiled. "I've been following these guys all summer. They closed down the Flying W, you know. I guess it got hot for them after you fell, and Nicky's over near Roosevelt selling 'used' cars and fixing the stock-car races."

"We're going to the races," I said, staring out at morning in the valley.

"Yep. Unless you'd like to call a lawyer and tell him everything and start and finish things the *right* way."

"That doesn't sound like a whole lot of fun," I said. "And besides, I had a lawyer before, I think. No, no lawyers. We'll get Lila to corroborate that I did not know what Nicky intended for my truck. Without her, it's my word against Nicky's, and that has had a tendency to fail. In addition, I have freshly escaped from a prison, and my credibility is full of dents."

As we talked I slumped in the car still pretending someone might be looking for me. I was confused at being ignored by the police. I must be lost, I thought, if they can't find me. I was sore from the attention the Waynes had paid me. I was impatient to have my name cleared. I wanted to see Lenore. Then these races. I envisioned Nicky and his crooked apprentices corraled at the drag races while the proper authorities patted me on the back, and shook my hand and the crowd applauded.

"Yes," I said finally, "we need to do this. Gather them together and wrap them up at the races or wherever we can have the police and an intelligent witness or two and make things clear."

Decisions are not my forte, but as I said it I knew I was right. Eldon laughed the old laugh now, the helpless agreement that implied he was with me. I told him to call me if he ever escaped from prison.

As I changed clothes, the excitement returned. This was not your average experience. I had escaped from prison and was driving around town with my best friend. I wanted more people to know about it though, so I could whisper to someone, "Keep your mouth shut and you won't get hurt."

"We have two days before doomsday," Eldon said, driving past the university, "and you," he pointed at my nose, "need mountain air and fresh fish."

"Need?" I said. I had heard his line before, but never spoken to me.

"Yes: need. The season's nearly over, but you are traveling with one of the contributing editors of *The Guide to Fishing in Eastern Utah,* and I know a few places where you can reach out and hook a few large trout who have never seen anything but the underside of their own loggy neighborhoods. This activity will firm your body and clear your head. Succor."

"Does this mean you're aiding and abetting me?"

"Haven't I always?"

He always had, but it was odd hearing him offer me "succor," a word we always had used when talking someone into a fishing trip. We'd been accomplices on those missions, selecting one of our friends in need of a vital lesson in aesthetics and trying to save him with the fishing.

We'd load my truck, and follow the rituals: oyster stew at the Wagon Wheel in Heber, beer at the Commercial Club in Duchesne, Indian reservation permits at the Day-Night Market in Roosevelt, and then we'd make our victim, our student, catch the first fish.

Well, succor seemed an attractive concept, and I hadn't seen a live trout for a while, and we did have the time, and the

races were out that way, *so* I agreed to the fishing which is a
need and makes life possible in the modern world. I told Eldon
I had a few things to do first. I had to see Lenore and visit a
few other primal spots before departing for fishing and the
clearing of my head and name.

35

Eldon's automobile was an automatic with a cluster of
push buttons as a transmission left of the steering wheel. The
body was an off-white, well, red, I suppose, festooned with
carbuncles of rust. Rust in fact, was the theme. "You know
what they call this car?"

"A Barracuda?"

"A Valiant!" He laughed.

Eldon conducted the Valiant to the apartment and pulled
up into the alley in the rear. "Stay here."

"Stay here?"

"Yes. The police might be around."

I got out of my side. "The police will not be around. They
are not interested." I wadded my prison clothes up and threw
them out on the alley.

"What are you doing?" He said.

"Clues. I am leaving clues. The police need help, and besides, I think there should be some clues."

I followed him around and up to the apartment. It was eerie
going up the steps. This place, I thought. This old place. His
typewriter was on the table, a page rolled in the carriage. I read
a few lines of dialogue: two people on a ski lift.

"What is this?"

"Fiction." He smiled. "I'm getting back into fiction. A beer?"

"Sure." He handed me a Rocky Mountain. They hadn't changed the label. The freak still sat on the log.

We sat on that old furniture and Eldon told me about his fishing adventures, and about old Nighthorse, his new Indian friend, and I told him about Spike, and the morning lapsed.

"Where's Kenny?"

"At class. You two have got to meet."

"What do you mean?"

"Check the kitchen."

I went in and was stricken by the walls. They were papered with book pages, even the ceiling and the shelves. "You mean he's a freak?"

"Look closer," he hollered in.

I went to the wall and read:

> One autumn night, five years before, they had been walking down the street when the leaves were falling, and they came to a place where there were no trees and the sidewalk was white with moonlight.

"Oh my god," I said.

"That's right. He bought six old copies of *Gatsby*, took them apart and did the kitchen. He wants to do this room with *Tender Is the Night.*"

"What?"

"He already has three copies."

I heard the door open, a sound I remembered, the loose knob and latch, and a voice said: "Hey, Eldon!"

A light-haired kid appeared in the doorway. He gave the

impression of standing effortlessly on his toes.

"Hey. Kenny this is Larry; Larry, Kenny. He's a Fitzgerald scholar." Eldon rose. "Well, I'll load this stuff in the car and be right up." I watched him go.

"You like Fitzgerald, eh?" I asked Kenny. On the desk I noticed all the books I had had on the subject, plus ten or twelve others. I hated seeing those new books.

"Yeah, Eldon tells me you like his stuff too."

"What's his best story?"

"The best," he said waving his hand, "is 'Winter Dreams'; the worst is 'Family in the Wind'; the most underrated is 'Babylon Revisited'; the most overrated is 'Bernice Bobs Her . . .'"

"Enough, Kenny, good show." I put down my beer. "When was Zelda killed?"

"March. Nineteen-forty-eight."

"What was Scott reading when he died?"

"The *Princeton Alumni Magazine.* I have a copy of the issue that fell from his hands. Want to see it?"

"Christ." I looked at Kenny's blond hair cut above his ears the way Scott had his. It was all too much. He looked like David Bowie. "Why are you interested in him, Ken?" I really at this point wanted to know. He faced me openly and with that twisted, ephemeral, ultraconfident, optimistic, mistaken, and secret smile I'd seen last in the mirror, said:

"I don't know. It's all beautiful. His life intrigues me; the romantic egoist, all of it. And besides, I want to be the greatest writer that ever lived, like he did, don't you?" He went on a minute before Eldon came back and sat beside me, and we watched and listened. Kenny retrieved a scrapbook and journal he was keeping, and held it before us turning the pages like a teacher. I could barely look.

"Do you want to see these?" Kenny held up a packet of letters. They were from the woman who had been the switchboard operator at the inn in Asheville, North Carolina, where Fitzgerald had stayed once in the late thirties. The handwriting on the envelopes was uneven, as if they'd been written while riding in a car. I realized the woman was very old.

"Sure," Eldon said. "Larry wants to see all of it."

"No, Kenny. Thanks. We have some errands to run," I said. I had to get out. I took Eldon's arm. "Don't we?"

I escorted him out into the foyer. "Thanks, Eldon; quite edifying."

"Yeah, isn't Kenny a nice kid? It's too bad to think that in a few short years he'll ruin his life by walking away from his perfect fiancee and fleeing into a living version of a grade B movie."

I didn't reply. Kenny's eyes stayed before me, bright, vulnerable, hooked.

"Let's have no more lessons, Eldon. All right?"

"Fine," he said, shrugging. "I just thought you two should meet."

Eldon and I went down to the Valiant and packed, mostly slopping things in the backseat and trunk the way we'd always done. The major element in leaving for a fishing trip is *leaving*. Eldon had a rod for me and extra socks.

"Okay," Eldon said shutting the trunk. "I'm going to pick up nightcrawlers. Want to come?"

"No." As I said this Kenny came running towards us.

"Hey. I was afraid you guys had left." He handed me a book. "I have an extra copy of this, and since you're interested, I thought you might like to have it." It was an annotated copy of *Save Me the Waltz*, Zelda's book.

I sat on the fender of Eldon's car. "Thanks, Kenny." Eldon

raised his eyebrows as if to indicate he had no hand in this.

"Sure. Well, I've got a date," Kenny said. "Good luck with the fish!" And he bounced away like a person about to own the world, his stride a flight. I knew his kind.

"Kenny," I yelled, "read the biographies backward, chapter by chapter, he gets younger and younger and richer and richer!"

He waved from the corner and said, "I'll do it!" with such urgency that I was sure he would, probably later that day.

"Coming?" Eldon said from the driver's seat.

"No. I'll stay here. Pick up the papers and some vermouth, will you? Let's do this right."

"When do you want to leave?"

"I'll be waiting for you at Lenore's at ten," I said.

"Still bent on repeating the past, eh?"

"What else is there? Not repeating anyway. Just get the stuff and be there at ten."

As he left he said, "Don't get hurt, Larry."

So I went back upstairs and sat through the afternoon. The sun whitened the columns in front of the Sorenson building up at the university, then turned the windows golden, as I smoked and thought about the first time we took Lenore fishing.

36

She had been a primary friend of ours for a long time, coming to the readings and movies at the apartment for months before Eldon found out that she had never been fishing. In our eyes that was the perfect ticket. The next day we packed and picked her up near the Hub telling her we were going to Roberto's House of Omelettes for coffee. When we had driven past Roberto's without a glance, Eldon told her: "You need to go fishing." Her response was quite different from Ribbo's. When we took him fishing he had informed us that kidnaping was a federal offense and he hated fish. Ribbo had stayed in the tent both days eating Hershey bars. He ate them carefully, looking up from time to time to see if we were going to steal them from him. Lenore, when informed of her Uinta destination, had said: "Come on, really, Eldon? Fishing! Great!"

We had had an extra fishing license made out in the name of Blanche DuBois (a fact Ribbo had not liked at all), and when we pinned it to Lenore's shirt, she climbed into the metaphor so quickly I wondered for a minute who the guides were here. "Why, boys," she'd said, her accent gone in Mississippi, "Ah caint wait."

The next morning we had gone to the stream with her for the first fish. She stepped out onto two stones in the water and let her line down where Eldon instructed in the shadow of the bank. As I watched her hold the pole in her teeth while she rolled up the sleeves of my plaid overshirt which she wore, it crowbarred at the foundations of this heart. Girls roll up their sleeves. She took a fish directly from the hollow, and I watched her face move from surety to surprise. A photographic memory, as you know, is no comfort in this world.

At that time Eldon had still been sensitive about his injury and carried it around awkwardly, obviously, like an old suitcase; he let us fish alone that day. Lenore netted nine to my six, handling them competently, showing me the particularly brilliantly spotted rainbows, and noting what they'd been eating when she cleaned them. That night, as was ritual, we had sat around watching Eldon's characteristically tiny campfire fall into itself and reading aloud from Robert Service. Lenore was more at ease than we were, and I think it scared us a little finally to have a partner who was up for the every detail of a fishing trip.

By the time we came down from fishing in the early evening and stood in the dusty streets of Duchesne, and went into the Commercial Club to douse our throats with glasses of cold beer, my heart was unmoored and bumping against the dock of my ribs. My tendency now, as then, is to heed cardiac responses, and as we stood at the bar, I was what they call a goner.

When I saw Lenore on campus four days later, she asked when we could go again. I could only interpret that "we" one way. I left Eldon a note as to my plans, but didn't tell him she was going. I couldn't tell him. Do you see? I left him the note, the best incomplete sentence in English: "Gone Fishing." When I returned on Tuesday, he said, "Courting, eh?"

That seemed so long ago.

I stood and stretched in a room where I'd shown a dozen movies. I remembered that tentacle in *It Came from Beneath the Sea* crushing twenty pedestrians in San Francisco. In the near dark, the pages of *Gatsby*, the wallpaper in the kitchen seemed more suffocating than ever. I went down the stairs and out into the October air. I wouldn't need a disguise; no one knew what I looked like in the first place.

37

Outside it was twilight and everybody was going home. Up and down the block girls were getting into cars. Birds flew over in threes, nestward. Cars were just beginning to turn on their lights, and the marquees of theatres beckoned with their lines of flickering bulbs. The air was warm again and huge doses of the smell of leaves blew past. I passed two kids on the sidewalk hurrying along. One said, "Hurry up before it gets dark." Now there's a credo. For a confusing minute I listened for my mother's voice calling my name on the tactile air, calling me for dinner. Twilight, it still works, I thought.

I passed a group of citizens picketing an X-rated cinema. They walked in a tiny circle with their signs: DECENCY! and AMERICA THE BEAUTIFUL? The breeze moved the skirts of the girls, and in the luminosity of the fading sky and the street lights and neon, I realized that I didn't understand sex either.

Perhaps the biggest lie we're told as we enter the inferno of adolescence is that it will pass. The people who say this, obviously, don't know they're lying; they love us and are desperate to say something that might offer us the kernel of hope as we enter that violent region from whose bourne no traveler returns. Oh, sure, it ends: when we fall to the carpet in some doctor's waiting room or rush open-armed onto the front-end of a moving automobile, but otherwise it's a permanent affliction. My own glands have driven me around quite a bit on roads at hours I might not otherwise have seen.

I kept walking, step by step, avoiding collisions with fixed objects, trees, parking meters, even though I realized this kind of thinking is always muddying the waters. Perhaps I should interview somebody on it. As I thought of talking to Lenore, a person on this planet whom I knew how to cherish, and that's a word, thinking of sex seemed even more distracting, which I guess is a soft term for the chronic natural schizophrenia which for me was the result of living in a body. The trees were all changing at the fringes to red and yellow, and I took the hollering I heard from behind the houses I passed to be the scrimmage instructions of kids playing backyard football. The earth, I understood, was tilting on its axis. Final darkness came as a relief and I thought of nothing, just breathing, not even of rehearsing what I should say to Lenore.

Alice, Lenore's neighbor, met me in the entry. She screamed and ran back indoors. At last, I thought, relieved: I've been recognized.

As I knocked on Lenore's door, I saw Alice move her curtains to see if in fact it *was* me.

"Oh come on, Alice!" I screamed. "You crazy bitch. You've got secrets in your heart like the rest of us!"

Lenore opened her door while I was still yelling. She was brushing her hair and, seeing me, stopped mid-stroke and sneezed: "Larry!"

"Free again. I'm innocent, you know." At this point if I wore a hat, I would have taken it off and swept it before her. She motioned me in and resumed brushing her hair, not taking her eyes off me. "Freedom is such a precious thing," I continued. She put the brush down and we looked at one another. "Hello, Lenore. Can we talk?"

"Gary's coming by in an hour; we're going out."

"Want to talk for an hour?"

"Larry, I'm getting married in nine days . . ."

"I know. Congratulations. Where shall we sit, in here?"

"No. Come on." She led me out onto the small terrace. Her backyard opened onto the apartments' communal green. In the center of the green was a set of swings and monkeybars. We could hear kids out there saying "Watch this!" to each other. The porch light from next door just clipped the top of her hair in white, and we sat in the dark. It was obvious that I was talking to an angel. Soon, I thought, I must cease taking everything as a sign.

"What have you been doing?" she asked.

"Nothing. Making errors. Growing up, I guess."

"It takes a long time, doesn't it." This wasn't a question.

"For some of us." Everything I say lives very near the glib, and I added sincerely: "I'm sorry."

She didn't say anything, just held her chin poised.

"Eldon says that letting you go was my major mistake."

"How is Eldon? I like him so much."

"Fine. The best person I know, I guess. He's aiding and abetting me. He says letting you go was . . ."

"I know. I went to see him while you were . . . Do you want to talk about prison?"

"I want to talk about *us.*" Again she said nothing. Two radios were playing across the courtyard or one radio between stations, some distant noise in October.

"I always liked it, Larry. I want you to know that. I liked going around with you. But you live like you're in a barrel going over Niagara Falls every minute."

"I know," I said, considering, "I am." It always backs me up to find that others consider my prime strengths to be my greatest weaknesses. She had me; I had to counter: "I find it cozy and exciting. Oh Christ, Lenore, isn't it better than living above the pharmacy and going down at intervals to sell bromides, ointments, laxa . . ."

"Larry." Spoken firmly. "Gary is a good person, a very good person, and I won't . . ."

"I know. I know." I did know. "But does he give you, well, a thrill, honestly? I mean, there's room in my barrel."

Her sigh was more like a cough; she was very close to asking me to leave. One of the kids fell off the monkeybars and began to wail. It was a reprieve for me.

"Larry." Her voice was the voice of reason. She sounded like Eric Sevareid. Why couldn't her voice be full of love or money or anything else beside reason, that dread killer. "You make my every gesture a symbol, some big deal."

"It is."

"It is not. It is not. You want too much. I don't mean a thing by any of it. If I brush my hair it means I want my hair neat, out of my eyes and ears. You think it's heavy, romantic. You think it's some romantic ancient motion. It's tiring."

"Sometimes you don't intend anything, but nevertheless, these things transcend your instincts." The kid's wailing had broken into the deep gasps of the recently saved.

"You're crazy. Look; what does this mean?" She put her perfect finger in her nostril.

"Don't do that."

"I am, I am. What does it mean, Larry, come on. What does this mean?" She looked at me with her finger in her nose and I looked back at her dark face, her light hair.

"You're beautiful with your finger in your nose."

"Paugh!" She stood up and walked to the edge of her patio looking out to where children risked falling in the dark. It wasn't a whole lot different from what I was up to here. I stood and went to her.

"Does he honestly give you a thrill?" I waited.

"Yes."

"Come on! You can't think that it's going to be a keen life. I'll bet you never laugh with him."

"Is laughter all there is for you?"

"No, but it helps the rest."

"We laugh a lot."

"Sure you do. When? What do you laugh at?"

"Things." She was moving a bit from foot to foot now; that was good.

"Pharmacy jokes?"

"Books! Movies! People in restaurants. Gary can guess their names and occupations. He's clever, you know. We have a *hundred* games. I shouldn't—I don't know why I'm telling you this."

I nearly said, "I don't either." I was in the corner again, overhearing my friends bet against me; it was late in the fight.

"A hundred games," echoed. I didn't need to hear that. Suddenly my head hurt. I touched the lump with my fingers.

"I don't believe you," I said. "Come on, Lenore, say you never laugh."

"Larry, I'm going to marry him." She had me on the mat now, and lying there I could see the round, glaring faces of those in the ringside seats.

My wind was gone. I should have avoided any tactics in which logic could enter. "A hundred games . . ." Common sense is my achilles heel.

"Then tell me you don't want to go to Duchesne with me tonight," I said desperately.

"Larry, I remember Duchesne. I remember all of it; it was good. I loved you even though I didn't know what you meant. It was fun." We stood for a couple of minutes not talking. She turned. "I'm going to get ready now." I needed a gold hat, I thought, I should have worn a gold hat.

"Do you mind if I sit here? Eldon's going to pick me up in a while; we're going fishing."

"Not at all." She left and I lit a Pall Mall. There, Fitzgerald; there you go. The moment is over and all its romantic freight has spilled into a cowfield in the Midwest of night. Out on the monkeybars one kid called to another: "Jump!" I yelled: "Hey, don't jump! It's late. Climb down and go home. Your mother just called me, she's got a prize for you." I could hear them run away.

I dislike smoking in the dark, and I put the cigarette out. Behind me, in the apartment a girl who would always be mine dressed herself to go out with her fiance. It made me feel a little better that this doesn't happen to everybody.

She came back out in a while and I tried to avoid looking at her apricot-colored skirt and brown tweed jacket. "Gary's here. I have to go, but you stay as long as you like. Just shut the door; it will lock."

"Thanks, Lenore. Goodbye."

She left. I considered going out and doing a one-half off the monkeybars. A minute later she came back in.

"Larry, I just want you to know that your friendship has meant a lot to me."

"Did you tell Gary I was here?"

"Yes."

"Isn't he coming in to shoot me?"

"No. We want you to come to the wedding if you can."

"Let's not talk this way; I liked it better when we were arguing."

"I have to go. Will you come to the wedding?"

"Maybe, Lenore. I'll try."

"Thanks, bye bye."

I am not going to any weddings. It would be too much like

Huck Finn at his own funeral, and besides, I didn't like it at all that Gary didn't consider me dangerous.

38

Eldon picked me up at nine-thirty, and he maneuvered the Valiant out of town. "How'd it go?"

"You get the vermouth?"

"Right. Five bottles. Three Cinzano and two Tribuno. The better brands end in *o* you know. And I purchased the papers. So, how'd it go?"

"Well we've waited long enough." I said reaching over the backseat for a bottle. The backseat was strewn now with fishing gear, the papers, books, hardback novels, his and mine. I liked that: always ready fiction, trying for other worlds. "Want some?" I measured the vermouth into one of the glasses he kept in the glove compartment.

"No way. Too sweet. I think you're supposed to eat that stuff on pancakes, regardless of anything they did in Paris. Are you going to tell me how Lenore was?"

I sipped the sweet warm vermouth. "Mummm. Well, it was okay. I've been invited to the wedding, and not as the groom."

"Best man?"

"Worst. It doesn't matter; I'm not going."

Before we left the city I asked Eldon to drive me out to the Rodeo Drive-In. It wasn't the scene of the crime, exactly. I just needed to see it again.

As we drove, leaves were loose. They were moving everywhere in low skittering groups. They crossed the road in front of us as though magnetized to the pavement, then, once across, the leaves would flare upward in a dervish spiral and collapse. They were trying. The wind sucked and whistled in the windows. It was a lonely night, *the* lonely night, perhaps, our headlights full of leaves, and I was glad to be simply in a car, with the green glow of the dashboard light on my glass of vermouth and my friend driving.

There were no lights at the Rodeo Drive-In. We drove past it once and had to go back. Eldon eased into the gravel driveway and up to the abandoned ticket booth. Glass was broken and lay like splinters of ice on the ground. Several large plastic letters from the marquee also littered the area. Abandoned. Leaves blew through gaps in the fence.

"Wait here a minute," I walked away into the deserted parking lot. Hands in pockets against the chill, I walked over the rippled ground. The little valleys were full of leaves and old popcorn boxes. The screen was still standing, but I could see stars through several holes in it. The snack bar was a dark lean-to now. I walked around to the projection room anyway. When I peered in, a horse showed me its sudden teeth in a laugh, reared, and kicked against the back wall. I jumped back involuntarily, and walked in a broad circle around the shack until my heart subsided. All right. Maybe this was the scene of the crime. I was having difficulty, as I ran my toe through the gravel and litter in the dark, remembering what the crime had been.

I jogged back to the car.

"Nobody home?" Eldon asked.

"Nobody we know. Let's have a little of this fishing, eh?"

Eldon backed out and we began our trip into the mountains. He rolled his window down and signaled the last left turn onto the highway that would take us through Heber, across the plateau of Strawberry Reservoir, past Currant Creek, to Duchesne where we would camp for the night on the edge of the superior Uinta Mountains. Eldon signaled with his arm, despite the Valiant's blinkers. "I prefer hand signals, it indicates an involvement." He smiled. "People believe you if your arm is out the window."

We climbed in the dark up the sinuous highway of Parley's Canyon past the huge gash called "Runaway Truck Lane" finally past the summit, a deer waiting in every bush, a hunter in every tree, then onto the broad Mountain Meadow below Park City. It was good to be moving. Lenore's face was reflected in the windshield. Eldon assured me that our plans for meeting Nicky and his friends, whom I referred to now correctly as "the assholes," would work out. Calling them that made me feel better.

We listened to Herb Jepko soothe a caller from Ontario who had recently had heart surgery. Jepko runs an all-night talk show for lonely hearts, that is, people in general, and his soft baritone voice is always laden with benevolence. Most of his callers just can't sleep, an affliction that I know as the nation's worst crippler. People weren't able to sleep from Guam to New Zealand, but we were the only car on the road. The vermouth was warming things easily.

39

Stopping in Heber was part of our ritual. The waitresses at the Wagon Wheel Cafe were always farm girls out to earn some money so they could attend Utah State or B.Y.U. next year where their boyfriends already went. Eldon and I drew great solace from being around such wholesome individuals, and we always ordered oyster stew and toast, and asked the girls about their futures. We'd been in often enough to be remembered, especially with Eldon's helmet, which he removed and set in the booth beside him.

When our waitress came over Eldon looked in her face a moment. She was incredibly clean, her white uniform crisp even at this late hour, and her complexion signaled her affinity for fresh air and quantities of milk. Eldon rubbed his eyes. "Lord," he said.

I ordered.

"Yeah," he said, "this is why we came. It's starting, right?"

"Yes it is. This is one of the places that still works."

When she returned with the stew and toast, Eldon brought up Lenore again.

"So, I missed the top girl. Think." I looked at the clock. "They're parked in his car outside her apartment right now."

"Engaged people get invited in."

"Shut up, Eldon. Is that possible? Shut up. Do not interrupt what I think of fondly as musing. I am only musing."

"Does your musing include further plans?"

"I'm going to bind all the letters she's given me and send her all my books as a wedding present with instructions to have her babies read them."

"Oh hell."

"I'll settle for the affection she still bears me," I went on, "which is the same general love girls have for their former teachers."

"I'm glad I'm hearing this shit in person."

"But first I'll fish and nail Nicky."

"There's one sensible item anyway," he said.

After so much alcohol, I was lulled into a sense of well-being. When we paid, the waitress said, "Thanks, and be good." I loved that. They always told us to be good.

We walked out into the main street of Heber, Utah. It was midnight in the broad valley, and behind the one- and two-story shops of the street, I could sense cattle sleeping in every field.

Eldon pointed at a poster in the cafe window. It advertised the Demo-Drag Race Spectacular. The posters showed two cars resembling sticks of dynamite about to collide. Oh boy.

"You still think this will work?" I asked him.

"If we have the police there and perhaps a notary public or two. Nicky's ripe. He's been fixing the races all summer. He pours enough sawdust into fifteen old junks to clear the gears and hires disenchanted farmboys and Indians to drive them around for a few minutes in the race. He pays each one about ten bucks, and when the Lone Racer, Teeth, is the last car running, Nicky collects the prize money. Teeth, Hardell, and Gunn take turns winning. It's especially nice because the Bureau of Indian Affairs sponsors the races. The track is half on the reservation."

Eldon handed me six postcards he'd bought in the Wagon Wheel. "Why don't you write invitations to the authorities?"

I sat in the car, fluent on vermouth, and drafted the cards.

Dear Highway Patrol: This is the wronged and innocent Larry Boosinger speaking. Please be at the Uinta Raceway at noon on Thursday since there are some criminals in need of apprehension. I didn't know about the wire, honest, Larry Boosinger. P.S. Bring your large guns and tear gas.

Dear Roosevelt Sheriff, Deputies, and Posse in general, etcetera: Don't you want to be at the races Thursday when you find out that I am innocent and that Nicky is a crook in your own community? Think of it, you can nab him! No trouble at all, Larry Boosinger.

Dear F.B.I. and Supreme Court: Please don't hold any grudges because I escaped from your facilities. You are invited to meet me in person and swap stories on Thursday at noon at the Uinta Raceway. Please bring an eraser to clear my name. For truth, justice and the American way, Larry Boosinger.

I wrote three others to various Justices of the Peace, a title I like, and we posted the cards. Slipping them into the mailbox, I saw that on the reverse side was a color cartoon of a deer driving a convertible down the highway with a hunter strapped to each fender.

40

We drove up through Daniel's Canyon, and across Strawberry in the dark, onward. At four in the morning, we pulled off the road north of Duchesne and parked by some other tents. Throwing our sleeping bags out on the ground, we bedded down.

There was some noise from the nearest tent, a small two-man nylon job. "Come on, Mary." Then again, "Mary, come on." The pro side of some sad little debate. This continued, as it evidently had all night: "Come on, come on." Finally Eldon arose and walked over above the tent and said directly down to it: "Either Mary you come on, or bub, you shut up!"

"Hey!" There was a shuffle. "You're asking for trouble, buddy!" the voice came back.

"Shhh. I want you to shut up now. Molest each other quietly

or I'll step on your tent. My partner is on his first deer hunt since being released from the home, and he is fragile and needs his sleep." That ended it, and we slept for two hours until dawn and the chill rain.

It rained for a good while before I woke up and then for another long while before I really woke up and then even more before I considered moving.

"Eldon. Hey, Eldon. It's raining."

"Absolutely. It's good for the fishing. Keeps them down." My bag was much heavier with the water and I could feel the damp on my leg and a part of my back; it was starting to come through. Eldon said: "Relax. Now we will move in orderly procession to the car." He began to get up. I jumped out of my bag into the prickling rain, gathered my gear in an armload mess and sprinted barefoot to the car. It was locked. Wincing, I watched Eldon rise leisurely, adjust his helmet, put on his glasses and stand up in only his underwear. He spoke across to me: "Go with dignity." He folded his bag and clothes and strode majestically over to where I waited. "When it rains," he advised me as he unlocked the door, "go with dignity."

He started the car, turned on the heater which was cold but smelled like dust which was at least something, and steered carefully over to the nylon tent. When the tent was grazing the bumper, he looked at me and pressed the horn. A guy stood bolt upright through the tent, trying it on as a hat, jumping around bare-legged in a checked hunting shirt. His face clearly showed that he had heard the final clarion, and he bellowed crazily, not quite awake. Mary, we supposed, ran out the other end of the tent in a snaggled pair of bikinis, her hands awake enough to cup her breasts. She ran in a short circle, and then over to a camper and snuggled pathetically onto the running board like a calf under its mother. Eldon was still on the horn.

Finally he let up and backed away. By this time the guy had unlocked the truck and he and the girl had relocked themselves in. We could see their faces against the steaming glass.

"Dignity," Robinson-Duff said. "Go with dignity." Eldon waved at them, and rolled down his window in the rain. They lowered theirs an inch. "Didn't mean to wake you. Just got out of the home." Then he wailed and flapped his tongue. They were staring at his helmet. "Soorrrry!" he shouted as he drove back onto the road toward Duchesne.

This is a lesson I had already mastered: dignity dwindles. And I also know Eldon's attempts to stem this tide are exactly based on the same heartsick logic which has caused others to place their thumbs in dikes. It only works in stories.

The lesson I had not mastered at all was that young women running around confused in the rain without dignity, clothes, or the sense to swear at tormentors, start the Lenore machinery in me. Just the old vast pangery; these are pangs, I thought, trying to breathe them off. I am always the person looking into other cars.

I turned the radio up to full volume. Dust bounced from the dashboard speaker in time to the Hollywood Strings' version of "Hey Jude"; I watched the fenceline all the rainy way back to Duchesne.

There I made Eldon accompany me over to the old Commercial Club.

"Come on, we're supposed to," I said. We avoided trouble by being the only customers that early in the morning. We'd had a couple of near scrapes in that room. The time we'd tried to educate Ribbo about fishing, he had insulted a ranch hand, and we had been forced into a three-man exit.

Eldon and I had two sticks of jerky and some pickled eggs for breakfast, along with glasses of beer the barkeep drew for us. We stood down the bar, as always, and made him slide us the glasses. Then he went back to mopping the floor, stooping occasionally to pick up coins or teeth from last night's festivities. The beer was the top of a new keg and effervescent; it eased my stomach and opened my head. There was a new sign behind the bar and it nailed me: WHEN THINGS GO WRONG, DON'T GO WITH THEM. We had two each, enough to bring back a colossal Lenore memory, and to open our eyes in the new sunlight outside the joint.

We turned north for the reservation and Nighthorse's house, where Eldon had spent a good deal of the summer.

41

Every drugstore window in Roosevelt was covered with the dynamite posters about the Drag Race-Demo Derby Spectacular.

At the Day-Night Market we went in to purchase our reservation permits as always and stood in line behind eleven deer hunters dressed for Viet Nam in green and brown camouflage fatigues. A couple had added the fillip of shoe-polish to their faces. Eldon asked me if we should tell them the war was over, and I asked him back if he was sure it was. The hunters looked at his helmet, and I could see them wonder if perhaps he had found some new deer-lure. One guy looked, through his shoe-polish, strongly like Salvatore from the prison laundry. We exchanged glances like pointed fingers, but since he didn't extend five, I didn't say anything. I was pretty sure it was he, but when we came out, the hunters were all gone.

We gassed next door to the Day-Night. A kid came out, his blond hair shooting from under his greasy green John Deere hat.

"What you got there?" Eldon pointed to a lowered, window-less '59 Chevy parked aside the garage. It was obviously the car whose tailfins had inspired the SST. On the side was a huge hand-painted numeral: 12.

"You ever heard of a stock car?" The kid swiped across the windshield with a rag.

"What do you think this is, friend?" Eldon continued to surpass himself. The kid was walking around the Valiant now, appraising it, wiping the windows occasionally. I winced in memory of my own self-destructive window-washing days, when Lila would moan and rock in her auto.

"Hell, this ain't bad." He looked at Eldon's hat.

"Correct." Eldon walked the kid over to the Chevy. "Who do you drive for?"

"What do you mean?"

"Good. I work for Nicky too." Eldon went back deep into the garage and emerged shaking up a spray-paint can. He kneeled outside the faded red Valiant and began spraying. I stepped out to see this.

"You drive for Nick, too?" The kid was amazed.

"Sure. Only this time (just between me and you) I might be going for the win." Eldon stood up from his artwork. It was a slanted "88." "He's not quite paying me enough to ditch this sweet mother." He opened his arms as if to embrace the rusted car. "Name's Rocky; what's yours?"

"Russ. Russell Case. Glad to meet you."

Eldon circled the car like a pool player figuring his next shot. He sprayed an "88" on the trunk and another on the passenger side. "I like the number, don't you?"

"Sure."

Eldon came back around and punched the kid playfully. "I like it because it reads the same upside down which is how I finish a lot of these here drag-race demo spectacles. Ha. Ha. Eh, Russell Case? But this time," Eldon handed the kid the paint can and we entered the car, "I'm going for the win! See you day after tomorrow!"

Eldon floored it and threw just enough gravel to anchor Russ's eyebrows in doubt. He turned to me. "The seeds of dissension. Did you see him check my helmet?"

"Upside down, eh?"

"Sometimes."

We passed the Jug Hollow Resort, a large tourist inn run by the Utes, one of the few Indian-owned businesses. It was shaped like a mountainous wigwam and featured a pool and a golf course. A gigantic Indian statue stood out front holding a tomahawk aloft. The Indian would have been a good rival for Allison Hayes, who played in *Attack of the Fifty-Foot Woman*, a film which no teenage boy should be allowed to witness. Across the face of the tomahawk it said: WELCOME ENGLISH DEPARTMENT RETREAT. I slumped in the seat and moaned. It was a valid moan, sounding evidence to the fact that there were some emotional powers I had not yet lost.

Five miles further Eldon stuck his arm out and turned left onto a dirt road which we followed for ten miles, raising a rolling trail of dust behind us. Another left turn put us on a two-rut road that ascended through a forest of aspens, green and gold with October. After fording a stream that washed the hubcaps, Eldon pulled up in front of a series of shacks annexed like spokes on a wheel. The air here was green and gold too. It was openly a fall afternoon, the sun soft and warm in the hills, the trees whispering, trading shadows right up the side of the mountains, into the high pines and the dark ravines and canyons, and then back down again under the aspens. Five thousand feet above us, north, I could see the new snow mixed with old on the talus running to the peaks of Gilbert and Emory mountains.

42

When we got out of the car we could hear piano notes coming from inside one of the shacks. "Mr. and Mrs. Nighthorse took care of me during the summer," Eldon said. "And now we're going to do them one favor." He went on to tell me about William Nighthorse who owned the only baby grand piano on the reservation. He had been a musician all his life, learning piano tuning from an old man named Levitre in Salt Lake, and as a teenager Nighthorse had played the piano and violin along with silent movies in Rexburg, Idaho. Mrs. Nighthorse taught piano to Indian children.

Eldon and I leaned against trusty old 88 for a moment listening to the piano notes falling around us. He removed his helmet and put it on the seat and replaced his glasses. His ears, ultrapale, white, bothered me as do most small porcelain objects, things that if you drop, you must purchase. The fringe of his hair was darkened by sweat. The music focused for a minute as Nighthorse, himself, stepped out of his shanty looking like Basil Rathbone. He was the first seventy-year-old man I've ever met who was six foot six.

"Writerman!" Nighthorse laughed and shook Eldon's hand. "And this must be Larry."

I shook his large hand. "My wife has a student right now. In awhile we'll go in for refreshment. Would you like the tour?" He had a scar from his left eye to the corner of his mouth.

"Larry needs to see the fish," Eldon said.

Nighthorse put his fatherly arm around Eldon and they led me around the house, on a dirt path, through a flourishing garden. Nighthorse paused and pulled three apple-sized radishes from the end of a row. He rinsed them in a narrow clear bypass stream and handed us each one. We continued through an aspen grove and up the path across a meadow. I could hear running water. We hiked up a short incline under the first pines and stood at the edge of a small pool. Nighthorse pointed at the middle and I could see the teeming backs of a thousand trout climbing into air.

"What?"

"This is the Nighthorse Hatchery." Eldon said. "Come over here."

Below the green pond, Nighthorse had three basins the size of bathtubs and in each, one monstrous trout. Lunkers. They lay in the bottom, not moving as has always been the prerogative of the monsters in any species. I guessed each at about eighteen pounds.

"Red. Buster. Sammy." Nighthorse named each. "They stay. Pets. Buster has been photographed eleven times."

"He was on the cover of last year's *Guide,*" Eldon added. "He's a beauty all right."

"Check Sammy's lip," Nighthorse said.

I kneeled and looked the big fish in the face. His lower jaw was separated in three places, testimony of his ability to avoid the frying pan.

"Handsome fish."

Bill Nighthorse did not comment. He was watching dust that was circling and rising and circling again above his empty corral. The whine of an engine flapped up to us, and through the dust we could see a fenderless hot rod sliding around the corners of the fence. The driver was making a reasonable attempt to catch his own tail. We watched him make four more furious laps, then dizzy, spin out, reverse, back out of the dust ring, jump up on the roof of the car, down to the ground and bury his head in the hood.

"Junior?" Eldon ran his hand through his fragile hair.

"Yes."

Junior resumed his racing, zooming this time the other way, to unwind, I suppose.

On the way back to the house, Eldon tossed the last bit of radish into the fish pond and there was a suitable uproar, trout climbing on each other like seals on a rock.

Eldon explained that Junior was Nicky's newest protégé, reconditioning used cars with the Waynes, and now he was one of Nicky's drivers. Bill Nighthorse himself said that he never interfered in the lives of his sons, but he was a little concerned about Junior, his youngest. Eldon promised the senior Nighthorse that we would woo Junior back to common sense, a domain I hoped we too would arrive at soon.

As we entered the dooryard Mrs. Nighthorse's student, a young girl with dominating braids, was leaving on the back of her brother's motorcycle. Mrs. Nighthorse came onto the porch and greeted us. Eldon fetched his gift copy of *Architecture West* out of our cluttered backseat and presented it to her.

"Hello, La."

We went into the manifold shanty to a sitting room adjacent the grand piano, as was everything else in the clean residence. The walls were all bookshelves, and the furniture modern.

There were no antlers on the wall, no wagon-wheel coffee tables. These Indians are letting me down, I thought over my glass of vermouth. Nighthorse and Eldon had martinis and we chatted about Junior's new enthusiasms until Junior himself came home. La asked him to sit and play "An American in Paris" for us as the afternoon failed.

After dinner, La's quiche and asparagus, we all had a pleasant roundtable in the den, another annex. Junior, his black hair still bearing the furrows from his comb, spoke animatedly about his "career" as Nicky's employee and the driving opportunities it afforded. Bill Nighthorse sat arms-folded in his leather chair smoking Riordan cigarettes from France.

"He's part Indian himself," Junior said.

"Who said?" Eldon asked.

"He did." Junior was hooked.

"Can you tell people you drive for him?"

"I'm supposed to be an independent."

"Suppose it's crooked?"

"It's a stock-car race," he said, standing up. "Nick helps me out." He went outside and we heard his car, wheels and a throttle, in a seizing cough that grew wider, ate the house and, swallowing, was gone, narrowing as he moved to the highway and the bright lights of Roosevelt. This vibrating show of fidelity added to my awe of Nicky. I was beginning to think of him as I think of the federal government: large, amorphous, and everybody I was meeting worked for him.

"Don't worry, La; Bill," Eldon said. "This boy can be made right. He'll be present at Nick's demise."

"I hope so," she said. "I hope so. It is not the purpose of my home to be a place where my son and husband can argue." Bill Nighthorse sat calmly, smoking.

La played the piano and sang a long song about wind and

vistas. I liked being reminded of these larger distances, the broad basin of eastern Utah, the Uinta Mountains, the only range in the United States of America that runs east and west, a genuine Continental Divide spoiler. The only thing about La's song that nagged at me was the reference to the future in every chorus. The future; life goes on and we get an opportunity to make the same mistakes twice.

When Eldon and I rose to leave, it was dark. Nighthorse came out to the car and handed Eldon and me white envelopes. There were four flies in each. They looked like pheasant feathers. "Thanks," he said. He sealed my fingers shut again with his handshake.

Eldon put his helmet back on. We'll see you at the races. We'll be the men with the moustaches in number eighty-eight."

43

Like any stock car, Eldon's Valiant high-centered three times on the high switch backs of the logging road that led us finally into a clearing about midnight. On the way up we listened to a radio drama which was about marriage and embezzlement, and to the news of circus animals biting people in the Denver airport. It is hard to believe there are no more circus trains to derail, allowing people to run from lions in the streets of their neighborhoods. Now it all happens at airports. It was fitting that we should high-center; we were cruising around the Uinta Mountains at about twelve thousand feet. I'd get out and rock the car while Eldon gunned it on the forward tilt, and the Valiant would slough off the center hump in the old road leaving a scar and a smear of oil.

Finally Eldon stopped the car in an opening in the trees. The clearing was an old log-loading station. A tremendous ancient scaffold leaned to the moon, and the whole area was cushioned by sawdust. The trees here were all new, about seven-feet tall. Eldon built one of his small fires—"Not enough light to get shot by, hell, this is Indian country"—and we had a camp. I erected a clothesline, and hung a towel on it. It looked good hanging there in firelight. The air was cold as stars, but I knew I had to sit up awhile and read the papers and have vermouth. Some things have to be done right.

I selected the latest, the top of the stack, the *Duchesne Register*, and sat near the fire, bottle by the neck, reading the set type of yesterday's news. Eldon was in his bag. He turned over and leaned against his helmet as a pillow.

I read the rodeo standings. A guy named Regan Vanderwoeden was in all around first. His calf-roping time was 7.1 seconds which I recognized as exactly how long coitus lasts between undergraduates. There was a photo of Vanderwoeden flipping a pained calf. This is when the goddamned paper caught fire, the fire surprising me with its large orange bites, and I hopped up, spilling the vermouth, and bunched the paper in a still-burning wad. Vanderwoeden and calf were smoke now, and I threw the whole bunch on the fire as I backed away. The flare woke Eldon who turned, his face white in the light, and said, "Oh, arson, now eh?"

Christ, you can't even read the papers. I climbed into the sleeping bag . . . And in my old sleeping bag, a good sleeping bag of canvas with a flannel liner adorned with a wallpaper pattern of bears and turkeys not a speck of down or nylon near me, I felt pretty good. The air was sharp, but the smell of sawdust soft, and the brook fell beneath me. I thought I'd seen

Vanderwoeden before. I think he worked with Panghurst in plates at the prison.

44

In the still, cold of the morning, I opened my eyes and between two trees caught the aerial photograph of the Great Basin sweeping purple and green in first light to the horizon and the first little steps of the Colorado Rocky Mountains. There was one cloud in a holding pattern over the tiny cluster of Roosevelt.

I sat up in the sleeping bag and righted the picture. Eldon was boiling coffee to a brown foam in a dented tin pan. I would catch fish today, and things, if not resolved, would at least be better. Eldon fried some eggs and Spam which we ate, sopping the grease with hard rolls.

"Our appointment with Nicky and the law is tomorrow at noon, so let's get going. It isn't a whole lot of solace, but it beats going to the dentist."

"I'm ready, I'm ready."

"Don't you want me to pan fry a few flapjacks so you can construct onion sandwiches and fold them in your shirt pockets for lunch?"

"Enough Eldon. I'm ready to catch three fish to your one. We may have read the same books, but I can see we came away with different things." I set the last section in the pole he loaned me, lined it, tied the hook on, and snagged it back through onto the reel. We had belt cans for worms and I had Nighthorse's flies in my pocket.

"Okay, Young Boosinger. The fishing is up and over from

here." He pointed. "Don't go out of the timber. The two streams run fairly parallel." He went on with his plans and verbal mappery, and we made arrangements to meet at a mythical spot he described on the far stream where three trees had fallen across. As I nodded "Yeah, okay," I knew I wouldn't be able to find it.

Eldon cut across then to intersect and fish up the Iron Fork. I walked around the camp for a while, savoring our little household in the forest, the sleeping bags, the rocks ringing the ashes, the clothesline, the empty cans. I drank the rest of the coffee, cold, right out of the pan, slopping a stripe down the front of my shirt, and began hiking straight up, saving the stream as long as I could.

Over the knoll above our camp, I entered the lost dead forest where the loggers had harvested every stick to timberline years ago, and I dodged the stumps in the gray land for about a mile, gradually ascending. It was eerie and good, and if it weren't for the massive wreckage, I would have sworn no men had ever been there before. In front of me ten miles I could see the bald noggin of Mount Gilbert bossing the other mountains around.

Colorado shimmered for me every time I turned around. Breathing became a campaign issue. I stopped and sat on one of the dry stumps, and took the packet of flies out of my pocket and examined them. They appeared the same, but looking closer I could see Nighthorse had made the eyes different colors. Maybe he was an Indian after all.

Finally, a breath for every step, I moved into the glowing forest, shade bright as air, floor soft as sawdust. I began climbing to my right through the widely spaced pines and rose up over a hummock. It was good to be the first man in the world again, and as I walked through each new room in the forest my reserves swelled.

Beside a boulder the size of a semitrailer on the hilltop I could see my stream drawing the silver line for its little valley. Walking, sliding, down the slope, the needles four thousand deep and golden under my feet, cushioning each footfall, the air slanted up now into my head, and I walked easily by the ninety-ton boulders, the furniture of the high woods. I passed through one grove of high pines and boulders, the trees not branching for seventy feet, the gray solemn rocks all square as houses, their shadows the size of European countries.

45

I first learned the value of being lost in the woods from my father near Spirit Lake on the other side of the Uinta Primitive Area. When I was eight we'd tour the lake in a rowboat, hunched in huge coats, sucking on lemon drops and fishing. He used two hooks and would catch one trout then wait to say anything until he had the second one swimming on the line and then say "Oh, oh." That was his signal, a soft: "Oh, oh, Larry." And he'd bring two amazed trout up to my amazed net. "You're not kidding anybody by only using one hook."

We'd limit early in the afternoon; he always let me catch my own fish. Then after cleaning them, we'd hike to one of the small upper lakes. It would rain every day at four as the new shipment of clouds ran aground on mountains higher than they'd anticipated, and my father and I would hunker in the pines looking at our pocket knives.

One year there was a sheepherder on the last meadow on the

top of the upper rivulet of the Black's Fork, and we spent the rainstorms with him in his tiny wagon which smelled of blankets. He talked the whole time it rained about the Jolly Roger in Evanston, an odd hotel. When we left, we hiked for two hours along the stream, teasing the small native trout with worms larger than themselves. Finally my father said not to worry about the sheepherder, that he was only lonely, and we walked out onto the last lake plateau, above the clouds. There was not a fish in the lake, and we walked around it slowly looking at the magnified rocks in the bottom, so recently released from ice. There was rock snow at the upper end, not a tree within a mile and the vast rocky talus amphitheatre of Mount Warren, not a single fan in the four million seats.

He always made sure we were "lost" on the way down, leaving the stream to follow a ridge that became two as the trees thickened, then two more, multiplying into a dozen alluvial toes. "Oh, oh, Larry," he'd say, "we're lost." The sun would be behind Warren now, two hours of daylight remaining. "I'll follow *you* out." Then I'd take him up and down the ridges, surprising the small deer asleep beside damp logs, once in a while noting an eagle gliding below us, until we came to where the stream should have been. It would've moved by then, and that is when I was lost. My mistake would seem ominous. My father would walk us down the vale fifty yards to a trail, finding an Old Timer pocket knife once, and in three minutes we'd be walking down the safe, known corridor of the stream, pausing at the pools to argue about which side to fish since it was twilight and shadows were not a factor. We'd debate for three minutes and then he'd drop a line in his side and pull a flipping fingerling right out. It was always as if he had a deal in advance with the little fish. Once in a while I'd step on the grassy bank only to find my foot falling right through the overhang into the water. We'd walk into camp at the stroke of dark; I was always wet to the waist. He'd hang my trousers on the clothesline, fry the trout which I'd eat with my fingers, the oil healing every scratch on my hands.

46

I stepped up to this stream as it flowed across a meadow full of wild iris spears and skunk cabbage. It was wide and even here, rocky and shallow, so I moved up along the soft bank to a rock the size of a taxi-cab which was parked strategically enough to send the water back and around, forming a small pool.

I quickly hooked two ten-inch Rainbows out of the pond now, and placed them in my creel. The bottom of my creel was still lined with paper clips and ball-point pens. Red ones. The residue of my scrape with teaching. I'd given marks with those pens. I tapped the final shudder out of each fish with the side of my Forest Master pocket knife and laid them in the creel with three wet iris leaves. I wasted twenty more minutes at the pond being toyed with by some creature who left only minute teeth marks on the worm.

Upstream the ponds were spaced every thirty yards or so, knots in the rope of the river, a dozen trout tied up in each. I had six when I came to a larger pool which faced against one sheer rock cliff, and caught Sammy's young nephew napping in the shade. When I saw the two-pounder, I knew his father had to be right above. The stream, however, moved into the walls of rock forty feet tall, and I had to back down and hike around and above almost a mile where it entered this canyon. It was dark in there and I wanted those fish. I crossed the stream four times trying to wish my way in. Finally I stood on a skull-size rock in the center of the stream and peered into the cave which narrowed at its top to about the wingspan of a crow.

The sun was speaking directly to all concerned from its perch in October, and I could feel the hair on my arms blonding. This is life on earth, I thought, for which I have perhaps too great an affection. In a month in the city a haze which will want to become frost will halo every streetlamp above the heads of football players as they walk home in the dusk. Now at 10:00 A.M. on the edge of the world, it was hot. I rolled my sleeves another turn. Wearing clothes, khakis dried to their righteous stiffness on the line, oxford cloth shirts, walking around the planet, avoiding prison in its deadly mediocrity by keeping good company and commiting simple deeds that reside between the legal margins: I want these things.

I was climbing above the narrow chasm through which the water streamed. When I reached the top and caught my wispy breath, I could again see the United States flying over the edge to the Louisiana Purchase (1803). Most of the abyss, that opened on the stream fifty or sixty feet below, was narrow enough to jump across. I was on a broad shadeless rock shelf. Following the edge I came to a point where it opened. I looked down at the stream. It widened, too, in the pool I'd been searching, an apartment house for big trout. I lay on my stomach and stared down through the smooth water to four shadows on the bottom. I always see the shadows, but can never see the fish. Riddel had taught me a name for this phenomena in philosophy. It was one of the fideists' central proofs for the existence of God. You can see the shadow and not the thing. Watching the immobile shadows, each the size and shape of the football that rested now behind the seat of my truck, it was proof enough for me. The sun clipped only half the pool, so I knew there must be about twelve fish sleeping below me.

I tied on a size larger hook, and threaded a fat worm over the barb, crimped a two-ounce sinker two feet up the line, above the leader, and lowered the line fifty feet and eased it into the water. I measured the depth as best I could to be about five or six feet, and watched the sinker raise a dash of sand off the bottom. The worm swam up, off the bottom, and began mingling with the shadows. I hoped they were fish. Philosophy only tells us that they *might* be.

I baked for a while lying on the rock shelf, staring down. Time to angle, I thought. I am now going to angle. I drew the pole a foot upstream and saw the sinker drag up a little sand on the bottom, and then without seeing a thing, I felt the pole buckle in an arc which should have snapped it. The shadows were gone, which according to philosophy means "fish on!" The line ripped its razor rip around the pool once and then I did see a tail tap the surface and splash downstream. I stretched my neck over the edge watching the line move to forty-five degrees as the fish carried the hook down, until I felt myself slipping, both arms paddling air. Whoa! I grabbed the pole again and moved back by knee-power.

I jumped up then and walked the tense pole down the crevice, feeling all the while the strong, even pressure of the fish as he took line off the drag release. It was too big a fish to go very far in this stream. Like people in cities who eat themselves into their apartments, becoming too large to ever exit again, these fish had come upstream in their younger, leaner days, had eaten eighty billion mosquitoes, and now they lived leisurely lives of retired gentlefish grazing in the two or three pools large enough for them.

This particular monster dragged me down the rocky steps with a force that made me question his age. I clambered down, following the pole, like a man carrying a safe; the choices were not mine. When I reached the last rock and stepped again into the woods above the meadow, I felt the confusing slackness, and reeled in until the pressure took line again, this time upstream. Climbing up again was nasty acrobatics. I tried to keep the pole over the stream and the line away from the sharp rock wall. He toured me, as I knew he would, right back to the hole where he had bit the hook, but I still couldn't see him. He continued upstream a ways as far as I can tell, because just as the line began to slant that way, I felt the electricity go off, and my line tailed up to me like a strand of hair.

It had sawed off on the rocks.

Examining it closely did not make me feel like an expert, nor did it make me feel any better. I looked back down at the water. The sun had moved and more of the ravine was in darkness, but I could see three shadows returned to their niches, like gems in a setting, fixed on the bottom.

"Wait here," I said straight down to them.

To seal the promise I knelt and laid one of Nighthorse's flies on the rock shelf; I would be back.

I walked up the rock sidewalk. At the first convenient spot, a place where the stream came out of another brief meadow, I collapsed on the bank and lowered my face to the water's surface. I drew two long draughts of the cold water, then dunked my whole head and drank off the bottom. It was headache cold, and revived my competitive spirit. I would live.

Glancing again at the sun, that mad traveler, I noted that I had time to net three more before climbing the hill that separated Eldon's endeavors from my own. I stood up, reconsidered, and knelt to drink again.

The water cycle, like all cycles, amazes me, and I was glad
to my arteries that this water had evaporated from San Francisco Bay, sailed east, fallen as snow during the Viet Nam war,
and now an eon of melting later, filtered through these woods
right into my mouth. It helped.

I fished two more holes above the meadow, not fooling
around, setting the hook hard and taking the fish five or ten
seconds after the strike right out of the water and introducing
them to air, bright ungillable air. They were the same size as
the others I'd caught below, and I laid them in the creel. When
I had the second one, I wet my hair again, and crossed the
stream, and climbed the hill hoping to catch sight of Eldon's
red hat.

From the ridge I saw nothing. I climbed the next, sweating
now in light that suddenly became slanted into afternoon. The
third ridge revealed the Iron Fork. Upstream half a mile I
found the unmistakable landmark of the three fallen trees that
formed a substantial bridge. I couldn't see Eldon, but when I
tied my creel to a limb under the bridge so it would depend
into the water, I saw his gill line. There were six fish on it; we'd
tied. Knowing then that Eldon had to be watching me, I
remounted the bridge, sat down and lit a cigarette.

"Come out of the woods whenever you find it convenient,
you wonderful, wily, sneaky Indianlike veteran. My blood deep
sixth sense tells me you're lost in your own primitive meta-
phors."

"You mean you want lunch, right?" Eldon called down from
his platform hideaway in a tree. It took me a full minute to spot
him.

"Trees," I said.

"Right this way, bub." He jumped down and led me to a
shady grassy part of the bank above the bridge where a minis-

cule fire was about to go out. He stoked it and fried the two fish he'd been hiding, the two that put him ahead of me. When they began to fall apart on the flat tin he used as a pan, he handed me one on a pine slab, and I sliced two thick pieces of cheese.

"We're going back over to the other fork after a while."

"Why?"

"I found Sammy and Red's brother, maybe their father, and I need a net man."

"Just a minute." He rose and went to the stream and returned with two dripping tin cans. He opened one and handed it to me. "Here, I brought you these." I looked down at a cluster of apricots. He saw my face and said, "Aiding and abetting."

"Thanks Eldon." I sucked one out of the cold tin. The apricots were cool and sweet and met each of my several internal miseries directly.

"Is it working?" He waved his hands across the forest as he leaned back against his helmet.

"Yes. I believe it is. Lenore's wedding shower seems two hundred and eight miles away."

"It is."

We lounged around on one elbow for awhile, smoking, talking about the time we tried to teach Ribbo about the woods. He had been unable to believe there was no electricity.

"Have you written about these forks for the *Guide?*"

"No no. You don't write about the good streams, the rare ones; that's suicide. A writer without a few secrets is out of gas. Besides, our readers prefer to fish from the back steps of their Winnebagos in little waters like Pelican Lake which I mention frequently. There are no hook-ups here, no snack bar, no propane distributor, and the fish are native. My readers prefer their fish hatched in the hatchery, properly, and flown in by Forest Service and dropped like little parachutists into the center of the lake. Any dolt with a year-old jar of fluorescent salmon eggs can snag them and fling them into the stainless-steel confines of his portable kitchen sink, which the fish in their confusion seem to prefer. I write for the modern outdoorsperson. People who climb this high to fish only read Twain, and Howells." As he spoke Eldon scooped out a hole and buried the cans. I smothered the gray remnants of our fire.

"Let's go fishing," he said. "Where is this hole full of giant fish?"

"Over three hills." I pointed. We gathered our gear and fish and started up the first incline.

47

The fly was where I had left it, but the ravine and pool were lost in shade now. Looking down we could see the rippleless surface of the dark water. "God, quite the place for sailfish all right," Eldon said. "There are fish down there that haven't seen the light of day. Probably albinos."

"Let's bring one out, eh?" I said.

I lowered a worm, again, down, way down into the stream. Nothing. I jogged it a bit. Nothing. The sun was softer now, awash in the trees, ready to be eaten by Mount Gilbert.

"Bring him up and try this." Eldon handed me a fly as I reeled in. While I changed gear, Eldon tied a yellow nylon cord to his net and lowered it in practice. I was suspicious of this long-distance, remote-control fishing, but the thought of net-

ting Sammy's brother or anything weighing eight pounds carried me onward. I lowered the fly to the surface. We couldn't
even see it. The net hovered five feet above the water. "It's all
by touch now." We lit our cigarettes and we sat down, dangling our legs fishward.

It was the strangest fishing I'd ever done, and I sat on the
strangest perch in time I'd ever known, and I looked off into
the woods below us which were beginning to stir with the
creaturings of late afternoon. The greens lapsed into blue as the
trees descended to the horizon; faces were formed and changed
expression in the millions and billions of boughs. I could make
out Scott Fitzgerald's profile, the famous one, the perfect one,
from the backs of his books. It glimmered in the distance as
he was turning his face toward us, I shifted to Eldon, who was
studying the pond below.

"You say you saw fish in this chasm?" Eldon asked.

"Their shadows," I said.

He looked at me in the dusky light and stood up. "Let's take
their shadows back to camp and fry a few for dinner."

While he was speaking I felt the line seize. It hopped and
went taut, running upstream. I didn't say anything. Eldon was
picking up his gear. He turned to face me. "Let's go."

Then he saw the pole, bent in a hoop, and I said: "Oh, oh."

"Holy shit!" he yelled. He threw his stuff down on the rocks
and whipped the net line free and lowered it again.

"Ease the drag. Give him line."

"That's how he sawed it off this morning." I set the drag.
"We're going to hoist him into the net *now*." We got to our
feet. I held him to the pool hoping the six-pound test line
would not snap. Eldon was trying to steer the net over the
splashing, but it was like trying to grab a dime out of a grate
with chewing gum on a string; there wasn't a whole lot of

purchase. For twenty minutes, we walked around as he swam the bottom of the pool. It was impossible to lift him while he was so strong. Eldon kept the net a foot off the water, ready.

"He's waiting for the sun to go down, so we misjudge and step over to our deaths."

"It's worth it."

The sun was behind Gilbert now, and we entered the extended high mountain twilight. Behind us, a crescent of the distant horizon was still golden in the sun, but crumbling like dry sand.

Eldon said, "Perhaps this fish has bears as allies who will venture out to bite us in the dark."

"Perhaps, you should hold the net at ready," I said.

"It has been ready for an hour. Let me know when you're through sporting, and I'll go to work."

The circles the fish swam were less frantic now, but just as steady. It was getting dark.

Eldon asked me: "Do you know what 'trout' means?"

"Oh yes. From the Greek: 'trouter' or 'truth.' " I pulled my rod into the bow again, no use. "Right?"

"To gnaw. It means 'to gnaw.' "

Then the line was dead. I took up line. We couldn't see but I suspected he was swimming the surface; the last cycle. "Put the net in the water."

"Where is the water?" Eldon said as he looked into the black hole. The pole bent again and line ticked off the drag.

"You're in; you're in! He's scared."

"We can't net him; I can't see anything."

"Faith, friend." I took line. He was tired. "Put your line parallel to mine." He held the net adjacent to my line.

"Okay, I felt him bump the net."

"I'll pull him out and you sweep him up . . . now!" Surprisingly, I lifted until the weight multiplied, became real in air, and I could feel the fish winging his tail in the air. The pole was insane with bending. Grabbing the line in my hands, I discarded the pole and began hoisting him up. Eldon was swinging the net back and forth randomly, chuckling at the measure of sensibility in such efforts. Finally he gave up and drew the net up quickly, holding it then in his hand. My line was like wire, I could feel it breaking every next second.

Eldon scooped the fish and nearly went over. I grabbed his arm with one hand, my other frozen on the fishline. The trout stood before us in the dark, arched into the sky like a god, his tail in the net.

"I don't believe this." Eldon said.

The fish moved, wriggled in unified strength. It was like holding the heart of a giant; its squirmings were seismic, pulsing above us. Eldon lost his grip and I went down onto rock. My hands lost the gills so I hugged it, trying to hold it with my cloth shirt. We rolled cheek to cheek like lovers, its tail slapping and punching my stomach convincingly.

"Hold him! I don't believe this!" Eldon scrambled. I got to my knees and looked at the fish. "He's a hundred years old!"

We knelt over him and I killed the fish. He had clearly been born in a previous century. Back at camp, he weighed out at eleven pounds.

Eldon mixed and warmed some powdered milk, and heated some cream of mushroom soup to make trout chowder, while I fried fillets of the fish. He laid the others in the ice. Sipping and scooping the soup into my mouth, breathing steam into the chilling air, sitting on my sleeping bag, tired to the corners of my lungs, dirty and warm as the fire shrank into trembling coals and my pupils widened in the dark, I was glad again to be associated with such a temporal, febrile object as my body.

We smoked Eldon's last two Lucky Strikes.

I could see Scott Fitzgerald lounging just out of the circle of firelight, his cigarette held glibly in two fingers. He was forty-four. His knit tie fell outside his worn coat. He smiled without opening his mouth. I nodded. I want to be innocent again, Scott. I want to be eleven years old in a rowboat behind the best man on campus, listening to him propose to a girl more beautiful than any woman in the world, my imagination gone on reflections in the water, peopled by giants and princesses, not a single compromise in the atmosphere.

The fish chowder had cleared my head.

I once dreamed he came to my desk with a copy of *The Last Tycoon* finished, and then we were walking through the abandoned alleys of Salt Lake City. After I had the dream, which was occasioned by half a quart of Beefeater gin at a reception for a visiting poet, I spent ten days wandering the side streets after midnight, searching. On the tenth day I stepped on a man's hand. He had been sleeping under some back stairs behind the Rialto, and woke to look at my saddle oxfords and then my eyes. I wrote in my journal that I had at last glimpsed the devil.

Now outside our circle, Scott Fitzgerald, a man eaten alive by his conception of romance and desire to be drawn inexorably up and toward the lights, the mainstream, seemed content to smile at me. It was the smile we offer children, and it is a promise that someday they'll know more than they do today.

Eldon dropped his cigarette in the fire and turned to slip into his sleeping bag.

"Did you see the fish?" I asked both of my friends.

"I'm still not sure," Eldon said.

Fitzgerald's eyes squinted almost to laughter; it was a joyous, derisive look.

"What happened?" I looked straight at him.

"Your imagination bit you," Eldon said. He knew me.

"Yeah, I guess so. Old movies. Summers when I was eleven I watched every late show there was. Did you ever see *I Married an Angel?*"

"Sure. That panorama of heaven, my first glimpse."

"People took their time. Things mattered. Mr. Smith went to Washington."

"No one should see that until they're thirty."

"And when my mind was ravaged by old movies, a silver screen of ninety heroes, I read the books. *This Side of Paradise* when I was seventeen. I learned how to smoke and moved my bed under the window. I was ripe."

"Yeah," Eldon said. "Well relax. Don't worry. We're the last victims. There aren't any good movies left and no one reads books."

"I'm not so sure."

"I am. Kids don't even read the labels on the drugs they swallow."

"You're a cynic."

"Yes, and you're my friend."

48

And so fine friends, readers for instance, one life becomes another the way morning becomes electric (I know, I know), the way night becomes morning, gradually, suddenly, and the changes surprise us until we're tired and lie down to change for the last time. What I mean is we left the mountains, a setting and viewpoint far above others I'd known, and raised dust on every switch-back and hairpin down, down, down, down. Ahead and below us, I knew the races could not quite measure up to a fish I'd seen and eaten. We'd had the climax over a river in the dark, and my innocence and proving it seemed less significant. Besides, I felt guilty again for not fishing more, for dragging four tons of self-pity to the Uinta Mountains.

Eldon leaned forward and shifted an imaginary stick shift in the Valiant in his crazy simulated test-pilot berserkness. He sang motor and brake sounds through each curve. We slid off the mountain sideways, or so it seemed, through the national forest gates and onto the flatlands where citizens for hundreds of miles around gathered their children into the family automobile and headed out for the raceway and the green flag that would drop near us at high noon. Footraces were started with a pistol, Eldon reminded me, because of the days when slaves ran away. In his helmet in the morning sun, motoring through Roosevelt in number 88, all six cylinders about to expire, Eldon looked the part: a cocky, deranged race-car driver.

"How you feel, Rocky."

"Wired. Primed."

"I'm Scared."

"Relax kid, it's my car that enters its last golden day on the laps of distinction."

We listened to the distant static of the Roosevelt radio station. The announcer left the tail-end off every word he spoke in some incredibly consistent suffix phobia as he introduced a Leon Sanger tune: "Horse Trailer Love." I was beginning to dislike this kind of massive country-western imprecision.

We lunched early on sausages and vermouth. Eldon sipped a little of the warm wine to further prime for the coming mangle. He pulled in the gas station next to the Day-Night

Market and filled the car with water, oil, and gasoline, putting an extra quart of oil in the rubble of the backseat. Russell Case and his stock car were already gone, and we could see the new yellow green color of the June grass under the spot where the car had been. We gave the nine remaining trout to the woman who pumped gas and she nodded her toothless thanks. Eldon never stopped at the self-serve pumps preferring the human contact, and "Besides," he'd say, "we're a self-serving enough country." I lowered all the windows and tied the doors shut with two neckties I located on the floor of the backseat. Eldon borrowed a crowbar from the woman, and said to the car, "This is going to be the hard part, Prince." While he climbed onto the hood, the woman asked, "What are you going to do?"

Eldon held the crowbar aloft, fifteen minutes from racetime, and looked at me. "Aiding and abetting. It's going to be worth it, I keep thinking." He tapped a small hole in the upper corner of the window and then levering the whole thing with the bar pulled it out, a rubbery spiderwebbed piece of broken glass, and dropped it to the ground.

"I need air when I drive," he explained to the woman. She held her breasts up with one arm and her chin up with the other hand. He then walked over the roof and broke out the rear window. "There! Now maybe a fellow can breathe."

"You don't fool me," she said, "You're in this stock-car race."

"Right as right," he answered, "Rocky's the name." He handed her the crowbar and we climbed through the windows into what remained of the Valiant. "Thank you kindly, ma'am. Just fry those fish in a little butter."

49

One way to create a sense of fall holiday when out for a drive in October is to extract the windshield from your car and let the fresh air blow directly, as it comes off the hood, into your passenger's mouth. Eldon and I motored along in this fashion toward the races. The air was redolent of cut hay, apples, and a little oil exhaust from our leakage. The last and largest and hardiest of the insect tribe bumped themselves against our squinting faces. Finally, at over fifty miles an hour, it became impossible to breathe facing straight ahead, and I had to turn my head or duck under the dash as if I were trying to light a cigarette. Eldon was laughing maniacally and swerving slightly from line to shoulder on the roadway.

"You're not driving," I yelled at his red helmet.

"What?"

"You are not driving in this race!" I repeated.

"My car. I drive." He slowed but not much, to make a right, and I could hear all the valuable trash in the backseat slide over. I held my door handle.

"Untrue, big boy," I said." I am going to drive us directly to the police who will be there and then to Nicky and Lila who will be there, and we will dismount, and things will settle."

"And you'll get your innocence back." He laughed. "No, I think I'll drive around in old eighty-eight today while you have conversations with Nicky."

Then we saw the grandstand, and I didn't want to be there anymore. There was a sign on an old snow fence RACES, with an arrow pointing straight into the sky. Overhead, one cloud crossed its fingers and became a Jolly Roger. A half-dozen birds made wing for Phoenix. I did not want to go near Nicky or the Waynes who would battery and assault me, and I did not want to go near the police who would replace me in the facilities. But we continued. Cars were parked randomly, a wheel in every ditch, in the nearby fields. Adrenalin was arriving to do my thinking in October.

"This might not work."

"It's all we've got," Eldon said. "And besides, we're here; it's so convenient."

There was a larger sign on the parking lot fence: DEMO-DERBY DRAG RACE TODAY! SEASON FINALE. Eldon cruised through the parking lot past two hundred cars and campers, and eased up to the inner gate marked PIT AREA—TRACK. We drove through.

"Hey!" The guard yelled and ran up to us. Eldon continued to let the car drift a bit as he talked.

"Howdy, howdy," Eldon said.

"You can't go into the pits." The guard held the door handle as he walked along with us.

"How have you been, Dave?" Eldon said.

"Malcolm."

"Right, Malcolm, sorry."

"You guys got a pass?"

"Hey, Mal, come on." Eldon stopped the car short and quickly pulled off his helmet. "It's me. Rocky." Malcolm squinted at him as if he were a math problem. *"Rocky,"* Eldon assisted him, "Nicky's *brother* for Christsake. Now get back and guard the gate before people start stealing cars."

"Oh, hell *Rocky,* I'm sorry, I . . ."

"It's all right. Where's Lila? I've got a present for her."

"They're in the infield like always." Before Malcolm finished saying this, Eldon drove away, nearly desocketing the guard's arm.

"Nicky's brother," I said.

"Something like that," Eldon said, replacing his helmet. "This is where we commence playing by ear."

The pit area was almost vacant. Several former automobiles relaxed on their sides and tops, clearly intent on never running again, and the gravel itself was marked conspicuously with the recent oil spoors from today's preparations. Screwdrivers and wrenches lay mingled in the grease, as testimony to haste. As we drove toward the opening in the cinder-block fence which bordered the track, a man stepped out of a camper and looked me flush in the face.

It was Wayne Gunn.

He snarled and took off at a run for the track, waving his arms and hollering: "Nick! Hey, Nick!" And before I could stop myself, I was out after him. He did not reach the track; I tackled him from behind, and lost myself fully in choking and punching this one-time table wielding antagonist of mine. I realize now that it was one of the few times in my life I have achieved that higher state of consciousness known as frenzy, and I don't regret it at all. By the time Eldon pulled me off, I had subdued Wayne Gunn somewhat. He was bleeding from the nose, and blinking so rapidly I thought I might have damaged his central nervous system, if he had one. He had stopped calling out, and his mouth only flickered in the rapid Morse code of the super-angry.

"Isn't that great?" Eldon said. "He remembers you." We lifted Gunn and placed him back in the camper, locking the door.

"This strikes me as one of the best things we've ever done," Eldon said. "You have to escape from prison more often."

We could hear a loudspeaker from the track instructing all the cars to back up to the starting line. That's right, I thought, they start these demo-derby spectaculars backwards; it's as sensible as anything else. Then the voice was encouraging bumping, crashing, and general collisionry, but no headons. *Good luck* the voice said. If those were the rules, we'd be all right; we'd been operating under the same principles for days.

Eldon nosed the car up to the track, and the thunder of the stock cars became specific. In the infield we could see Nicky and Lila sitting on top of his Volkswagen bus in deck chairs. They were enjoying beverages from a thermos. Also, we could see seven squad cars representing the various law enforcement agencies we'd written to.

"They must have received your cards," Eldon said. "Now just go over and begin a rational explanation."

I scanned the scene. It seemed so right and so wrong. I could sense the process of lawyering beginning again, and I didn't want that. I wanted to punch and throttle a few more old friends and lock them in campers.

"I don't know," I said to Eldon. "Why don't you go across and do the rational things?"

Behind us there was a rush and a scream, and we turned to see Wayne Gunn lunge for me with an axe in his hand. Eldon moved out, and Gunn swung, imbedding the weapon in the trunk instead of my head. We dragged him ten feet before he let go, and then Malcolm was helping him up.

"What is this, serious?" Eldon yelled as he swerved onto the track and drove a quarter-mile up to where the other cars were backed, ready to start. "Are they going to kill us?" The axe stuck straight up like our scared tail.

"Should we go home?" I said.

Eldon didn't answer me. "All right, then. Let's have a stock-car race, boys." He laughed the old uncertain ha, ha. And he slipped on a pair of leather work gloves.

There were three rows of five cars all backed now to the starting line and we were in the middle of the last row. Looking next door, I saw Junior Nighthorse pumping his hot rod into earthquake vibrato. He looked back at me, his mouth closed tightly. All around us there were race-car drivers prepping for damage, gunning blue grey clouds of oil smoke at each other. The sky went dark and the earth from where I sat smelled like the last automotive holocaust.

I shrugged at Junior and mouthed: "Nicky's a crook!" His rod exploded back at me: Rrraaahhrrrr! It rocked on its wheels like a boat against the current. I couldn't hear the Valiant at all, and while two men stood on a scaffold near the track and scanned a clipboard and pointed at us, Eldon jumped out his window and kicked our muffler into pieces. "That's better," he said, getting back in. Now the Valiant sounded its challenging roar against the distant hills; actually, it made a noise like something alive going down a drain in the Great Basin.

The track itself had been plowed and watered like a cornfield to slow everybody down. It looked more suitable for bullfighting; it wouldn't be a bad idea, it struck me, to run the cars through the streets of Roosevelt, with a group of drunk and daring pedestrians fleeing before them, occasionally standing to wave a blanket at the headlights of the leader.

A jolt! We turned to see two feet on the trunk and then a face fell upside down into the hole where the windshield had been. "Hey! Rocky, how are you doing?"

We both cocked our heads to make out who was speaking.

"Okay, Russ, ready, ready."

"You still going for the win?"

"Nothing else. If they get this damn thing started."

I could see Nick pointing our way.

"Well, watch out!" Russell's voice was barely audible in the roar. "Watch out for me pal: I'm going to win too!" His smile, an upside-down celebration, spread across his face. We watched him clamber back through the top of his '59 Chevy which was directly behind, that is, in front, of us.

The stands were full of a thousand multi-colored shirts and from the havoc of our pre-wreckage r.p.m.'s the entire grandstand seemed to be swaying in waves, like gelatin.

So we have it all, as a man raises a green flag; a round dirt world with people finally ready for the climactic rinsing of my name. I saw Bill Nighthorse on the front row. He looked larger than anyone else around, like a judge at this little trial. He raised a hand to Eldon and me and his mouth remained even, a line, as if he knew it all already. He looked like everybody's father, saying, "We're lost," but knowing where the path was all the time. I liked his knowing. Things were drawing to a focus I appreciated. At last there would be multiple witnesses, and I scanned the seats further for another honest face.

Then I looked back through the smoke at the scaffold where a man held the green flag. I grabbed Eldon's sleeve.

"Junior wants to talk to you."

Eldon leaned across and hollered, "What?"

Junior turned, looking puzzled.

"What is it?" Eldon roared. Junior still could not hear.

"Go see," I urged, "But make it quick."

Eldon climbed out his window and ran around the car.

The flag dropped.

I slid over and gunned it, ignoring Eldon's screaming. All the cars jumped and sat for half a second digging a little place in the mud, and then we were officially off, backward as a group, bumping softly, fenderly into one another. Eldon ran up and

tried to jump on the hood of the Valiant, but too late. He fell
to his hands and knees, then stood up and pointed at me hard,
stiffly. "Talk to the officials!" I yelled, pointing at the police.

The pack remained just that, a pack, to the first turn, every
driver with his arm clutching the seat, steering backward, looking for the first turnabout possibility. I could see Darrel Teeth
in front, leading in a winding reverse. Right behind Teeth,
Wayne Hardell drove a modified '54 Ford cleverly labeled
number 1 and painted with hood flames. Hardell gripped the
wheel in ferocious apathy until he caught sight of me. While
I registered in his brain, and blood filled the fragile corpuscles
of Hardell's eyes, I pushed the D button, stopped in a skid—
and drove forward in a broad U-turn, becoming the first car
forward in the race.

For a minute I contemplated staying safely behind everyone,
but drivers were catching onto the tactic, and Junior swung his
car around. So I sprinted to the outside, sideswiping the yellow
DeSoto, taking the driver's door off. As the door cartwheeled
irregularly down the track behind us, I heard the first crowd
noises, and I wondered again about finding an honest reliable
witness in the whole wreckophilic bunch.

"Back in your seats!" I yelled.

Staying outside, in a minute I was in the lead. I might win
this mother. I saw Darrel Teeth with teeth bared at me as I
passed. He was sideways, turning his Mercury around, and Russ
had aided him considerably by ramming into Teeth's front
fender. Darrel bit his steering wheel, or seemed to, symbolizing
his mammoth desire to run over my head.

By now all the cars but one had righted themselves, and we
again bunched on the far straightaway. The track was soft and
deep with dirt clods, and I tried to send the twin spumes of
mud that the tires sawed into the air against the wicked surface

of Teeth's face. I could see him ducking. Everybody in the pack was eating dirt.

Wayne Hardell had customized his Ford a bit by installing something similar to the engine from a Lear Jet. While Teeth rammed me repeatedly in the rear, and the axe handle waved in his face, Hardell passed us on the outside. We all crossed the line for lap one.

Wayne then pulled ahead of me and closed what was becoming a grim sandwich. He looked around and his mouth made the *S* he substituted for a smile. I flipped him the bird. I mean there he was fifteen feet ahead of me; it seemed appropriate. He slowed to about sixty, and Lone Racer Teeth sped up to about seventy and I could feel the Valiant lifting, almost airborne.

They had me trapped. We took the first turn in this stuffy trio, locked like a train with a madman at the throttle. Hardell's exhaust and mossy breath ran through my car. Experimentally, I let go of the wheel; nothing happened. I put an elbow out the window and an arm on the seat and pushed the cigarette lighter in with my toe. I was not in control. For a moment, I wished I'd brought a lunch. When the lighter popped out, I ducked and lit a cigarette, letting the ashes flee generously back into Darrel Teeth's narrowed eyes.

In the infield I could see his majesty Nicky watching the races from his throne atop his van. I waved at Lila. Beneath them Eldon, helmet under his arm, was speaking to two police officers and pointing at me. I waved at them too and nodded wildly to agree with whatever he was saying.

I felt another jolt as Teeth touched up his speed a bit, and I reached into the back seat for a copy of the *Tribune*. I let each sheet go individually for a while and watched Darrell dodge them. The funnies stuck over his face, but only for a second.

Then our railroad ensemble was on the backstretch, and the

industrious and deserving Russell Case, thumb on nose, passed us all on the outside. I loved it. He was fishtailing in joy, throwing dirt in every window. Behind him, equally earnest, Junior kept pace. As a tribute to my credibility, Junior swerved and delivered me a mild concussion doorwise and was gone. I could have poked him in the eye.

Ahead in the track, I saw Russell and Junior sweep inside of one entrant, a stationwagon over on its smoking side. Hardell rammed it on purpose and tore the top off the wagon, jarring those of us in the dining car. One of the stationwagon's tires flew up and landed on my hood. I pulled it off.

Three other cars were disabled, and two of the drivers were frantic to get theirs away from the third which was frying in forty-foot flames. They hopped around the track uselessly, dodging the mad traffic which from time to time tried to bump them into the grandstand. Finally, two of the drivers lapsed into a fistfight in the infield. It was heartening to see two men finally pay attention to one another. In a way it reminded me of love; two people for awhile making every move in deep, lost concentration, acting as if every move the other person made mattered. One of the men, his overalls ripped into a Tarzan sarong, looked too much like Le Habre, a relief pitcher for the Escapees. The police moved the two dazed men apart.

I began honking occasionally at Wayne Hardell, who couldn't quite figure it out. "Move over!" I waved. "Russell's going for the win!" He ignored me, but I could see Big Nicky gesturing and swiveling in concern toward Russell's Chevy, number 12, which now had half a lap on us.

From time to time the crowd would exhale in unison, signaling yet another collision or rollover. The track was filling with used auto parts. An axle rolling on its own passed us all in the fourth lap.

But something was not happening that should. An announcer was not broadcasting my innocence for all to hear. This is it, I thought, this is supposed to be where it all comes to a knot tighter than our three-car traveling auto wreck, and I step out in a moment filled with the proper bystanders and surprised looks and point my finger—at Nicky. In that moment I am supposed to be believed, and then a hand larger and more official than my own sweeps down and erases my slate: innocent. The retractions are to spread from local paper to paper, and the airwaves are to be full of my reclaimed newness. INNOCENT MAN JAILED, CLEARED, REIMBURSED, LUNCH WITH GOVERNOR SCHEDULED. This was the plan. But don't so many of our plans grow whiskers in the moonlight, becoming dreams then nightmares that roam the countryside biting innocent people near Detroit?

In fact, something was happening that should not. Wayne Hardell was bookending my front-end, and Darrel Teeth in his daredevil mobile was giving me what is called the hard ride from the rear. I was keeping bad company at sixty-eight miles an hour. In this clogged environment, things were not clearing up. I spat back at Darrel Teeth; it splattered on the trunk.

In the infield now I could see a larger group of police surrounding Eldon. Then Lila and two other police joined the group. Eldon still had his helmet off and appeared to be directing the discussion. Nicky remained on top of his van, but he was waving his finger at Russell Case in number 12, and shouting. One of the policemen nearest Eldon was writing things in a small notebook while he looked our way.

"You've had it!" I yelled back at Teeth. "They're taking names!" He couldn't hear me.

In lap six, Russell and Junior, in that speeding order, began the mad tailgating and random rear bumping of Darrel Teeth. They were trying to lap us all and put the race on ice. Wayne

Hardell swerved our clattering three-car ensemble wildly up and down the banked track to block them. I could feel us accelerate, and pressed the brake. No use: Teeth was pushing too hard.

When we whipped around the last turn, and refocused on the grandstand straightaway, bearing down like the chased, Wayne Gunn blew out in front of us sideways in his camper pickup. The rear door was waving open, and the whole image was that of a cow straddling the tracks in front of a closing locomotive. The Waynes exchanged terminal glances, and for the first time I was glad Hardell was ahead of me.

There wasn't time to do anything; Wayne Hardell tried to turn up and strike the rear-end of the camper, but it didn't matter. I ducked and closed my mouth.

WHAM! Hardell's Ford went halfway through the camper body, spewing pans and silverware out in a bright fan. In the wind and speed, I rode the Valiant up his rising trunk in a flying jack-knife, and catapulted over their collision into the apocalyptic tailspin that would seal all deals.

It was hard keeping track for a while. I heard the metal scream as the axe tore loose and flew off toward other lives. Behind me I heard repeated explosions punctuating half a dozen racing careers, and looking up once, I saw my heels. I was in serious centrifugal motion, sitting on the roof being pummeled by Eldon's novels, smothered by papers; then on the passenger door, pulling my arm back in the window before the view became all earth. I saw the cop cars in telephoto view. The group of policemen and Eldon. Lila, jumping. Nicky's van did a closeup, and I slid, upside down on the roof, plowing a generous cut of earth into my lap. On the final turn, like a spinning bottle, the Valiant touched Nicky's bus once. Glass broke.

I looked out the side window to see Nicky, like a skier in a wayward chairlift, clutch the arms of his deck chair and go over the back of his van: Whhoooaaaa!

"Get out!" I yelled to Eldon who was invisible. I dug around in the dirt and rubble, throwing books and papers. I remembered: He was not in the car. There was a subdued belch and the Valiant was in flames. I skittered out the window and was helped to my feet by a patrolman.

"Eldon!" I screamed, spinning away from the officer: "Eldon!"

"He's over here, son," the cop said. There was no skin on my elbows. The temperature had changed somehow. My nostrils were full of earth. "Over here son . . . over here son." Son? My hearing was magnified, the volume swinging up and down. The eyes were afloat. I was standing up, I think, on the curved earth.

I found Nicky. He pulsed and waved in my vision like a mirage. He lay inert on his back. The particles of his deck chair were everywhere. "Tell him, Nicky! Tell the officer!" The mound of Nicky did not really move. He was unconscious or dead. "No!" I screamed. "Nicky!" Medical persons began kneeling around him. I slugged his van and cried, "Eldon!" It was more like a cough.

Then the sky was smoke in a vortex, flushing away to a pinpoint, and, above the blue lights on police cars snapping in their little circles, I saw Nighthorse. It was like a photograph. The freeze-action photograph in films where the action stops, and becomes a page in an album and a gigantic hand reaches down from heaven and turns the page. The picture was Nighthorse standing in flames above the heads of two policemen, his hands on their shoulders, my name in his voice, his head tangent with all the rafters of the firmament. The iris of smoke clenched to a close before I saw the giant page-turning hand.

50

I awoke in the back of an ambulance, I supposed, and passed out again when I saw that VanBuren, the Nevada Kidnapper, was driving.

51

The next view I had was white. Then three photos of Eldon's sister, Evelyn. I awoke the final time at three in the morning; well, it was dark and the clock by the bed said three. I sat up and was not as confused as humiliated by the twisted gown I seemed to have on backwards. As I set my own two feet on the cold tile floor I contemplated escaping from what was clearly another institution, the places I seemed to be leaving. I strolled down to the night station, where the nurse was cleaning out her purse. She had her personal knick-knackery out on the desk.

"Hello."

"Hello," she said, handing me a picture of a boy dressed as Peter Pan. "Mickey, my oldest. He'll be six this week."

"Great costume. I was always Robin Hood."

She looked at me.

"On Halloween."

She kept looking.

"I always went as Robin Hood. Once I went as Gary Cooper."

She finally nodded.

"Where are the guards?" I asked.

She looked at me again, saying nothing.

I backed away. "That Mickey's a fine-looking boy. You're lucky."

She watched me, so I turned and sauntered back to bed where I discovered sleep, heavy as earth.

Toward morning I had a dream of escaping from the orphanage. Eldon dumped his porridge on Miss Cranley's head and I broke the windows and then we jumped the fence and filled our pockets with apples. The horizon was a vast unending ribbon of light.

52

The next morning when I awoke the ward was quiet. The only other person moving was mopping the floor at the other end. I found my clothes, laundered and in a nearby locker, so I dressed and walked out into the lobby. There were no policemen, no teachers, no ex-convicts. I read a copy of the *Colorado Democrat* from cover to cover, including Eldon's article on the oldest democrat in the Rocky Mountains, and every time an idea seeped into my head, I fought it down with big sticks. Nurses and doctors came and went, ignoring me, which I took as a sign that something dire was about to happen.

It didn't.

I felt the pieces of my past and future all over the floor of my mind like eggshells, and I didn't want to think their correct reassembly was impossible. I wanted not to touch them with a single thought, until some competent, perfect soul would explain them into their proper places one by one.

At eleven, Evelyn and Zeke picked me up and I signed some papers for the nurse on duty.

"Where's Eldon?" My eyes moved in a dizzy focus and I had to shut them from time to time to stop things. It was like old times when I was up all night two or three nights at the power plant. The October light listed this late in the month, and the sides of everything were white.

"Salt Lake. He had a checkup and he's all right. He sent us."

"Checkup?" As I walked the blood seemed to be draining out of my head. I went to one knee on the lawn and put my head down.

"Are you all right?"

"Sure." I stood up again, but the blood stayed down and I went lax, doll's eyelids, into her arms.

"Larry!" I heard Evelyn say my name, and I smelled the sun in her hair, and then we had lying on the lawn for a while. Zeke ran around kicking things I could not see, coming over every so often.

"He's a white one, Mom, isn't he," he'd say.

"Should I get a doctor?" Evelyn asked.

"No, you stay. I'll get up occasionally and you catch me. I'll be all right." She sat beside me, her legs crossed. I watched her roll up the sleeves of her green plaid shirt. "What is this checkup?"

"He was bumped when you crashed."

"Bumped?"

"It's nothing. He'll tell you that you tried to run over him. One bruise, or something. He's fine," Evelyn said. Zeke appeared.

"You're white, Larry," he said. "Want an apple?"

He went away and came back with some red apples. Evelyn and I ate the apples while Zeke went back over to the front of the hospital and had a conversation with a cab driver. When he returned I felt better, and stood up easily. Evelyn took my arm, and Zeke walked before us explaining that a lot of women were having babies in that building.

When we reached the parking lot, Evelyn stopped. "I thought you might want to see this." She pointed at my green truck.

I couldn't speak for a moment.

"I remember this," I said finally placing my hand on the fender. It was warm from the sun. "I remember this." I slid in the driver's seat and every gauge came back. But the soft friction in my head continued, and when Evelyn said she'd drive, I let her.

Zeke wanted to ride in the back, but Evelyn said no, and so I offered to ride in back with him. "Air," I said. She smiled again. Zeke and I climbed into the back and he climbed onto my lap.

"We shined the truck, right Larry?" he said.

"Right," I answered. Evelyn drove the truck westward while Zeke and I counted ducks moving in the transparent sky.

53

Outside of Heber, she stopped at a roadside fruit and vegetable stand and allowed Zeke to select the pumpkin of his choice. We picked out several large squash and some apples, and I watched Evelyn drink a large glass of cider. When she saw me watching, she laughed and said, "Well, it's *good!*" We bought the cider and hoisted Zeke's pumpkin into the truck. He had chosen an asymmetrical monster, larger than a bushel basket. "Some pumpkin," he kept saying. Then he wanted to ride in back with it, but we decided instead to ride in the cab. Evelyn began explaining what had happened. Zeke kept leaning on my shoulder, turning back to check his pumpkin and then turning back to look in my car.

54

I was right about the race, Evelyn told me. It was no climax. It wasn't even an anticlimax. It was a dirty demo-derby spectacular in which undistinguished gentlemen in abused machines chased each other in elliptical circles always returning the way they had come. No one was killed. There were some fair concussions, including my own, however, and Lila had spilled the beans to the officials. Those beans led to an appointment I had in the Metropolitan Hall of Justice to sign six papers and exonerate myself. So in a vague way, I was cleared, though the air still seemed full of dust.

Nicky and his friends had been filed, as I was, in hospital beds and then asked to leave the county. None of *them* had even mentioned my name. No one had asked them. They had risen, at intervals, from infirmary beds and walked as American citizens to futures, like my own, not a lot different from their pasts. History teaches us that it does not teach us.

Nighthorse had claimed the ashes of Eldon's Valiant and paid the seventy-five dollars damage incurred when the axe that had been in 88's trunk had severed the grill of a Highway Patrol car. His son, Junior, due to Nicky's moving, would be unemployed for a while, which was all the time Senior Nighthorse thought he needed to get him an honest career. My eternal friend Eldon, after being bumped by his own car and his own friend, had proceeded to Salt Lake to see about his knee and to free my truck.

As Evelyn told me all this, the explanations seemed as distant and strange as if reported by a butler three days after a shooting. It was like reading about other people's woes in the papers.

So time had passed, regardless of anything I had done, regardless of anything Eldon had done, and I was as guilty or innocent as ever. I just didn't involve the police anymore. I can believe it.

I thought about that for a long time: innocence. No, there is no going back to that one, no matter how many circles one races in. I felt, as Evelyn drove over the last hill of Parley's Canyon and we stared at the urban grid of Salt Lake City, that I should move to a small community in Upstate New York and never be heard from again. I felt as though I should return to the safety of the Midwest where I had never been. I felt as if I had gone to great lengths to recover from my education. I felt as if I had just turned thirty. Actually, I felt that April was over, pretty much. I was just glad to have tasted that fish.

55

Yesterday we went to the Veteran's Hospital to visit Eldon, who is not hurt but is staying there for two weeks "recuperating" from a badly bruised knee and writing his next piece for *The Guide to Fishing in Eastern Utah.* We found him on the fourth-floor sun deck, wearing his helmet and sunglasses, and my old grey sportcoat over his pajamas. Zeke always greets him with: "Glad to make your acquaintance, I'm sure." Evelyn always holds his hand, standing by him, and he always shakes his head at me and says, "Junior wants to talk to me, eh?"

Then he asks me what my plans are and I tell him something different every visit. Yesterday: sailing. People are supposed to go to sea, I think. He tells me I should go on the stage where aberrant behavior is encouraged. I tell him watch out I might. Then Zeke takes Eldon's clipboard and tries to read it aloud, and yesterday Evelyn asked Eldon to dinner. He's coming tonight. Before we leave each time, Eldon calls over one of the other veterans and introduces me as the guy who ran over him.

56

Well, I've run over a lot of things, I suppose. The best had been the trustee orchard and the worst had been Lenore and portions of myself. I have thought for a long time that it was paramount, essential, to be the best or the worst. Partly out of the superlative viewpoints those extremes offer, the amazing vistas, the thrilling false euphorias, roads not taken, roads that, I guess, should not be taken, and especially because of the distances from crowds. The middleground is so goddamned crowded. To be like everyone else, yikes; that is the cardinal sin. That was what I had thought. Tonight I feel as if I've been taking the high ground so long that I am dizzy, fatigued, and in need of a map.

Nothing should be approached part-time, ordinarily, piece-meal, or sensibly; this is also what I had once thought. I do know that it is not that amusing when we first learn life to be the mile, when we've been running the hundred-yard dash. I'm looking now, I guess, for a new stride.

Perhaps I've made the first step. I went out tonight, earlier, and covered the tomato plants with burlap in anticipation of the second frost of the season. It seems a positive motion, even if I did have to have Evelyn show me how to do it correctly.

Evelyn and Zeke are visiting, and we await Eldon who will join us for charcoaled steaks and liters of red wine which are breathing on the trailer steps right now. My green truck sits patiently beside the trailer, my own home. The river is full and makes a sound like wind in high trees, and I consider time. That things require time is a concept I am just becoming familiar with.

It is twilight again; the shadows are about to spread and merge into that glowing version of first darkness. My recent past seems the meeting place of two confusing words: touched and touching: crazy and tender. Across the river the city skyline stands like a chess game. The rancherly dooryard is weed-thick, but the garden has been kept to order by Evelyn and Zeke while I spent my summer vacation in prison. Evelyn wears a white sweater tonight, a practical and lovely touch, a thing women do. I am just moving into its appreciation.

As we stroll around the ranch, I avoid stepping on the weeds and reflect. I've been into Fitzgerald and loss for awhile now, and pretty successfully it seems to me as I count my friends. I was the moth and he was the flame, and I can wish forever, which I undoubtedly will do (and plan on in a sense), but I can never reverse it. I would rather have been him than known him. I only wonder now if I can get into "regaining" or even find its advocate. One thing I won't regain is my degree. Let it go, I think. Having a degree ahead of you all your life implies a future, another concept I might flirt with soon.

For instance, I'm going to buy a piano which I will lean on and Zeke will learn to play. Evelyn already knows how, a blessing. And I anticipate times will again become sunny, lucky, and every pair of trousers I take off the closet door in the morning will have three dollars in the pocket, and eventually there will be a time when kids come up and drink out of the hose and I squirt the last one so he remembers me, and women I'm related to will bake cakes in the shapes of rabbits and bears and castles to celebrate minor occasions, such as my birth.

If I have converted my heart into a warehouse, fine. I peek in from time to time and have the pangs. If you challenge my ability to store pang-inspiring material, or think I am kidding, I am disappointed. All my life I have been plagued, which is a serious pestilential verb, by my peers, which is a silly name for folks my own age, who have mistaken my sense of humor as a frivolous quirk. It is, in fact, the central sense in Larry Boosinger's survival. It is the only sense I know.

I hadn't been a great actor, or soldier, or even the only other valid thing, a great criminal. I had been a Dangerous Convict which, as you know, is not quite the same thing. Oh, I blame Nicky and those guys who have not ever been properly squelched and are into some version of automotive crime even now, but as my father noted, my blame won't fix a lot. And in a way I'm glad I had the *quality* of trouble I had. Everybody allots thirty-five percent of *his* time to troubles and worry, heartache in general, and I would have loathed using my thirty-five percent on, say, being refused credit at Sears or not receiving my license plates on time, when I could have had prison. I really mean that.

And I don't blame Scott Fitzgerald. That would be wrong.

His were simply the most alluring, thrilling lies I'd ever heard. They still are.

I don't know about the final test; you know, where I meet Wayne Hardell coming out of the Rialto Theatre in three years and our eyes meet and we stop on the sidewalk and perhaps he puts out his calloused hand. Perhaps he's forgotten or grown out of his chronic venomous urges, and I will stand in this world, pedestrians flowing by on either side . . . And I will probably extend my own hand. Why not? Recognition is a compliment, and if it is true that one is known by his enemies, then I should think it proper that Hardell identify me.

In the kitchen sink hibachi the coals are warming satisfactorily, and Evelyn and I sit in the riverbound Studebaker watching leaves float by in shifting constellations on the river. Zeke trots around the yard waving his grape popsicle like a pistol, singing a melody that he makes up as he goes along.

A large, misshapen jack-o-lantern guards us all from the top of this old car; the candle glow just becoming visible in the dusk. I have not yet begun to court Evelyn, but I suspect I will in time, taking my time with new care. It is difficult to be perfect in this world, but I think there should still be attempts. If things don't assemble themselves similarly to the things in old movies, then perhaps they shouldn't. Zeke has found a horny toad and he brings it over on a leash he's made from string. "His name is Salt Lake City," he says. Zeke's hair is four cowlicks and a part. I've started reading again: *The Lives of the Great Composers,* and Zeke and I have set up an elementary school for one on weekends, and we're learning about the stars which are not at all the same. One of Zeke's first paintings is already taped to my refrigerator door. It is a house. You can tell because of a large green square which is a window.

While Evelyn and I talk about the coming winter, three men

I knew in prison approach in a canoe. They are dressed in denim and paddling hard like incensed Dutch sailors late for the discovery of a new world. Their eyes are full of wonder. Their mouths are open. A man who worked with Spike and me on landscape sits in the middle, lower than the other two. They pause a moment from manifest destinies, and, holding their dripping paddles aloft, this October, they wave.